2

Excalibur

2
Excalibur

Colin Thompson
illustrations by the author

RANDOM HOUSE AUSTRALIA

This work is fictitious. Any resemblance to anyone living or dead is purely coincidental, though if you recognise yourself in this story, you could probably go on one of those rubbish reality TV shows and talk about it.

A Random House book
Published by Random House Australia Pty Ltd
Level 3, 100 Pacific Highway, North Sydney NSW 2060
www.randomhouse.com.au

First published by Random House Australia in 2010

Addresses for companies within the Random House Group can be found at
www.randomhouse.com.au/offices

National Library of Australia
Cataloguing-in-Publication Entry

Author: Thompson, Colin, (Colin Edward)
Title: Excalibur / Colin Thompson
ISBN: 978 1 74166 382 2 (pbk.)
Series: Thompson, Colin (Colin Edward). Dragons; 2
Target audience: For primary school age
Dewey Number: A823.3

Design, illustrations and typesetting by Colin Thompson
Printed in Australia by Griffin Press, an accredited ISO AS/NZS 14001:2004 Environmental Management System printer

10 9 8 7 6 5 4 3 2 1

The paper this book is printed on is certified by the © 1996 Forest Stewardship Council A.C. (FSC). Griffin Press holds FSC chain of custody SGS-COC-005088. FSC promotes environmentally responsible, socially beneficial and economically viable management of the world's forests.

For Walter, who is probably
a fun-size King Arthur.

Bored

The trouble with living happily ever after is that it can get pretty boring, and for Kings and Queens and Noble Knights it can get ten times more boring than it does for ordinary people because they are ten times more intelligent than ordinary people.

Of course, in the olden days there were millions of things humans could do to stop being bored. The trouble is that most of them, such as pressing flowers or knitting tabards out of horse hair, were even more boring than being bored.

Peasants, being much more stupid, could find enjoyment in a stick – especially if it was a really interesting stick with an insect on it, or it had a bump that looked a bit rude – whereas aristocrats barely noticed sticks.

You would never have heard a Great Knight say, 'Oh my, look at the lovely reddish-brown bark on this wonderful stick I was lucky enough to find in the forest.'

The Knight would probably have said, 'What on earth are we doing in this gloomy forest where there isn't even a single wild boar for me to cruelly slaughter?'

Or –

'What stick?'

Noble Knights were above nature and all that sort of thing, especially if they were sitting on a very big horse, and particularly if the horse had just trodden on the stick and broken it into lots of little pieces.

When that happened the peasant would rejoice and say, 'Hooray, the Gods have sent me a small pile of kindling wood to light the fire to cook my simple evening meal of rabbit's foot stew.'

From the moment they got up in the morning until they collapsed exhausted into bed each night, peasants were simply too busy trying to find enough to eat, while avoiding all the scabs and diseases that peasants kept getting, to be bored. Being bored was a luxury they could only dream of and that didn't happen because they were so poor that they could only afford the very cheapest dream, the one about the potato peel and squirrel's bladder stew.

So throughout most of the countryside of Avalon there was very little boredom.

Camelot, however, was overrun with it.

A King or a Queen could do many things to

stop being bored. Money was no object so they could summon all sorts of wonderful things from far and near to entertain themselves with. If a Noble Person sitting on the very high walls of Camelot got fed up looking out across the lovely surrounding lake at all the lovely islands and the lovely swans gliding through the lovely water lilies casting their lovely reflections in the lovely water, they could simply send down for a few spotty urchins to toss over the edge and place bets on which one would drown first, or whether one would make it to dry land before Krakatoa the Giant Olm[1] reached them. The trouble was that that got boring too. And they kept running out of urchins.

Boredom was why war was invented. It was something exciting to do.

Of course, it's hard to imagine how anyone living in a country as staggeringly beautiful as Avalon – with its Quest of the Month Club, Kitty Jousting and endless towers full of Damsels in Distress – could ever be bored. People from less advanced countries such as Italy or Wales or Everywhere Else could only sigh and

---

[1] *See* The Dragons 1: Camelot.

dream of living in a country full of such fabulousness.

It is even harder to imagine that King Arthur, the ruler of this paradise on earth, would ever get fed up for more than three seconds.

But that is exactly what happened.

'Might I make a suggestion, sire?' said Merlin, when he found the young King twiddling his thumbs, his ears and the ears of three small kittens.

'Oh, yes please,' said King Arthur.

'Since it was discovered that you were the true King of Avalon, rather than that horrible boy who we sent down to the kitchens, there is something we have not done,' said the wizard.

'Yes?'

'Well, we were all so busy fixing the drains and sorting out the dragon problem,' said the old wizard, 'that we have had no official celebrations or even a coronation.'

'Do you mean a party?' said Arthur, untwiddling his fingers, ears and kittens.

'Indeed, sire,' said Merlin.

'Oh yes, oh yes,' said Arthur's sister, Morgan le Fey.

'After all, your highnesses,' Merlin continued, 'I don't think either of you, or anyone else, realises what a terrible downward path to doom our entire beloved country was on while that terrible little impostor was running things. I feared that even with my great powers to protect us, we would have been invaded and maybe even conquered by our enemies.'

'Wow,' said King Arthur.

'Indeed, we need to have a great coronation . . .'

'And a party,' Arthur added.

'Indeed so, sire, a great coronation and a great party are what we need to show the rest of the world that Avalon is once again a great power to be reckoned with.'

'So we shall invite those who may have thought to invade us,' said Morgan le Fey, 'and show them we are strong.'

'Exactly so,' said Merlin, 'We shall drink and feast and make lots and lots of merry with a fayre and the finest of entertainments.'

'Brilliant,' said Arthur. 'And we can show them that we have made a treaty with the dragons. That will stop anyone ever thinking of waging war upon Avalon.'

But all was not well in the Kingdom of Avalon.

As word spread that the bad fake King Arthur had been replaced with the genuine wonderful King Arthur, happiness spread throughout the land. Everyone was filled with a new optimism for the future. The harvests would be good. The weather would be perfect. Rain would only fall at night when everyone was asleep, and the plague of boils that had run rampant since King Uther Pendragon had died would give way to skin as smooth as velvet with only the occasional zit or blackhead.

Yet there were those who were not happy.

In the kitchens of Camelot there was a small boy who was unhappier than anyone else, a boy who wanted revenge: dark, evil, painful revenge with boils the size of brussel sprouts that always burst at the most embarrassing times. That boy, now called Brat, was the pretend King Arthur, the changeling who had been swapped at birth for the real King. He had not known he was a fake. He had assumed that he was the rightful King and not, as it turned out, the unwanted child of the nineteenth daughter of a lowly fifth-grade pimple-squeezer from a remote Welsh village with a name no one could pronounce because it had no vowels in it. He had assumed he was the King of Avalon and all he could think of was becoming King again. If it took death and destruction to achieve it, that would be a bonus.

'I am the innocent victim of a terrible miscarriage of justice,' he took to saying to anyone who went near him, but all that meant was no one went near him if they could possibly avoid it. Of course, most of the people working around him in the kitchen were incapable of understanding any words with more than four letters in them so they just assumed he was talking Welsh, which was another good reason to keep away from him.

'Shut up, Brat, you little worm,' said the Cook to whom he now belonged, 'and get on with your turnip gouging.'[2]

---

[2] *Turnip gouging is an ancient occupation that has largely become obsolete due to modern hygienic farming methods. It involved digging all the maggots out of turnips with a special tool. The only good thing about the job was that the gouger was allowed to eat the maggots, which were a rich source of protein.*

'But it isn't fair,' he whinged.

'And what idiot told you that life was fair?' said the Cook. 'If life was fair, I would weigh fifty kilos less than I do and would be lying in a bath of asses' milk while the incredibly gorgeous Sir Lancelot fed me chocolate-covered strawberries.'

'If you help me get the throne back,' said Brat the Pretender, 'that could be your reward.'

'Yeah right,' said the Cook. 'And how will I suddenly lose fifty kilos?'

I'll cut your stupid head off for a start, Brat thought.

Another thing he thought was, *Surely I can't be the only one who thinks our wimpy new King is not so wonderful.*

But it appeared he was. Everyone loved the True King Arthur, especially those in Camelot Castle who knew only too well what the Fake King Arthur had been like.

Brat was nasty, cowardly, self-important and seventeen other unpleasant things, but one thing he was not was stupid. He knew that to start a rebellion you needed more than one person. Not only that, the

other people needed to be mean and cunning, though not as mean and cunning as he was in case they decided they would rather be in charge instead of him. He also needed to recruit foot soldiers, people whose feet were cleverer than their heads, people who would be too stupid to realise the bomb they were going to set off would kill them too or the very well-armed soldiers they were about to attack with small sticks would probably beat the hell out of them. Those weren't so hard to find. All Brat had to do was find the people who were so thick and ugly and weird that no one wanted to be their friend or even go near them.

It hadn't taken much to work out that Scraper was such a person.

The castle kitchens were where the lowest of the low ended up working. This was where the creatures who were so ugly that it was illegal for them to go out in daylight lived, and there were beings far worse than that. In fact, if you had seen some of the stuff that leaked out of them as they prepared the food, you would never have eaten anything Camelot had to offer. Yet there were people who were below them – and the lowest of all of them was Scraper.

10

Scraper was the lowest person in the whole castle. Scraper was the person who cleaned the disgusting disease-ridden-anthrax-infected-lavatory-flavoured stuff from under the fingernails of the Sewer Cleaners as they slept each night. There were no tools for this job because they rotted away in a couple of days, even if they were made of the hardest steel. No, Scraper used his teeth, teeth that even the vilest bacteria ran away from.

Needless to say, Scraper was not in the top class at school. In fact, he had never been to school. His mother had sent him every day, but not once in twelve years had he ever managed to get there. He always got lost. He usually fell into a ditch and stayed there until the family dog arrived at sunset and dragged him home again. In the Olden Days, when there were hundreds of ditches everywhere, this could happen to anyone, but what made Scraper's failure incredible was that he lived in the schoolhouse, which was next door to the school – his father was the headmaster. It was because Scraper's father had taught one of the Sewer Cleaners that he managed to get his son the job, that and the fact that no one else was stupid enough to want it.

'How would you like to be a general?' said Brat.

'A genrul wot?' said Scraper.

'No, an army general,' said Brat.

'Army?' said Scraper. 'Wossat? Is it like leggy only it's your arm?'

Brat realised it would be a better idea to talk to a bucket.

'Wot you saying to my bukkit?' said Scraper. 'That's my bukkit, that is. No one else is allowed to talk to my bukkit.'

'I was telling her how lucky she is to belong to someone as nice as you,' said Brat.

'What she say?'

'She said to tell you to tell me that she would like you to be a general and be in my army of liberation and help fight the righteous rebellion,' said Brat.

'Gosh. My bukkit's a clever bukkit, isn't she, knowing them long words?'

'She is indeed. You're a very lucky boy.'

Brat thought that, with soldiers like Scraper, his chances of a successful uprising were considerably lessened.

But beggars can't be choosers, he thought. *The*

bucket might come in handy, and if I get shot at, someone big and lumpy like Scraper will be really good to put between me and the gun. All I need is another five thousand Scrapers and I can't fail.

'Tonight,' he said to Scraper, 'we shall flee this place and take to the hills.'

'Flea? I arn't got fleas,' said Scraper.

This was true, since any flea that bit him died in less than a minute.

'And what you taking them to the hills for? Aren't they got any up there?'

'Any what?'

'Fleas.'

Brick wall, head, hit, against, thought Brat, *would be more relaxing than this.*

'And get all your friends to come too,' Brat said.

'What's them then?'

'You know, a friend, someone special you like and who likes you. Oh, umm, doesn't matter.'

'Like my bukkit?'

'Umm, yes, or maybe another person.'

'I loves my bukkit.'

Some time after midnight, when everyone was

asleep, Brat packed his meagre belongings, and the crusts and gristle trimmings he had been stashing away for the past month, into an old sack and prepared to leave the castle.[3] He went down to the slime trap where Scraper was sleeping and shook him awake. Before the idiot could speak and maybe wake someone, Brat stuffed a knob of gristle in his mouth and dragged him up into the moonlight. This was all supposed to be swift and silent, but was actually slow and loud due to the fact that Scraper's left foot was stuck fast in his bucket. Brat expected to be stopped at every turn, but the sound of Scraper grunting through a mouthful of gristle, combined with the ungodly clatter of his bucket on every second stair, made those who heard the noise hide themselves under the bedcovers until it had passed.

Camelot Castle was overrun with spooks, ghosts, demons and the walking undead, which meant people usually locked themselves in their rooms at night and nothing could persuade them to go out. The next day, talk of the Clattering Grunter Ghost was all over the

---

[3] *His meagre belongings consisted of the old sack and a collection of toenails in a sow's ear he had made out of a silk purse.*

castle. Only the Cook realised what had happened when she found Brat was not asleep in his cage as usual.

As Brat and Scraper reached the line of bridges and islands that would lead them to freedom, Scraper grew silent and anxious. He had never left Camelot before. As far as he knew, the castle was the whole world and outside was darkness where the devil lived. That was what his father had always told him and his father was a teacher so he must know everything.

'Scared,' he whimpered as they passed through the main gate. 'Devil get us. Devil eat us and take my bukkit.'

'No,' said Brat. 'I know the devil. He's a friend of mine so he won't hurt you because you are with me.'

'What about bukkit?'

'Bukkit is a friend of mine too,' said Brat. 'And anyway, the devil's got his own bucket. No, you just keep chewing that gristle and grunting and put on this magic cloak that I've got for you.'

He put a filthy old flour sack over Scraper's head. With the bucket still on his foot and all the grunting, the sight and sound Scraper made was terrifying enough to make sure they crossed to the mainland

without a single sentry or guard challenging them.

'Listen, men,' said the chief sentry to his men the next morning. 'If anyone asks us, we didn't see a thing last night apart from a small tabby kitten that went by about three in the morning.'

And by the next morning the two runaways had travelled round the far side of the lake and climbed up to a small cave halfway up the mountain that looked down over the water to the fabulous castle of Camelot.

'One day all this will be mine again,' said Brat. 'Just like it used to be, only better.'

'Can I take bag off head now,' said Scraper, 'and swallow gristle?'

'Yes, yes, of course,' said Brat.

'I can't get bukkit off foot,' said Scraper. 'Walking made it stuck on.'

'Why was your foot in the bucket in the first place?' said Brat.

'Bukkit sleep on my foot to stop bukkit theefs stealing her,' said Scraper.

'Right.'

'Bukkit theefs come in night and kidsnaps bukkits, erryone noes that.'

'Today we will rest,' Brat announced. 'And tomorrow we will begin to make plans.'

'Ooh, I like them.'

'What?'

'Plans,' said Scraper. 'Specially the red ones cos they got the sweetest, but be careful not swallow stones.'

'That's plums, you idiot.'

'You make some tomorrow?'

Brat walked into the shadows at the back of the cave and hit his head against a rock until he felt a bit less desperate.

'You too, eh?' said a voice in the darkness.

'Who's there?' said Brat.

'That depends,' said the voice.

'On what?'

'On who you are.'

'I am the real King Arthur,' said Brat. 'Or I was until last week, when everyone ganged up on me and pretended I wasn't and installed a fake puppet on the throne.'

'I know,' said the voice. 'That puppet turned my dad into a jelly baby. Can you believe it, my dad, once the mighty King of Dragons, sworn enemy of all

17

humans, has formed an alliance with that puppet.'

'Are you a, umm, er, are you a dragon?' said Brat, backing away from the darkness.

'I am indeed,' said the voice. 'I am Bloat, son of Spikeweed, once the greatest Dragon King who ever lived, but now as noble as a baby rabbit in a nappy. Alliance with humans, I ask you. No offence.'

'None taken,' said Brat. 'But listen. It seems to me that we are on the same side.'

'But you're a human,' said Bloat, 'and I'm a dragon. We're supposed to be enemies.'

'True,' said Brat, 'but it seems as if right now, we both want the same thing. I mean, if I was King again, I can assure you there would be no treaties with any dragons.'

'I likes treaties,' said Scraper. 'Choccy-covered nuckles are best treaties. I likes them.'

'Shut up,' said Brat and Bloat at the same time.

'So what are you going to do about it?' said Bloat. 'How are you going to get the throne back?'

'I am going to do a revolution.'

'Well, I know I said dragons making alliances with humans was against nature,' said Bloat, 'but maybe

that's exactly what you and I should do. You know, just until you got the throne back again, only temporary.'

'Yes, temporary would be all right,' said Brat, 'just until I'm King again. Then we'd stop having the alliance and be enemies again.'

'Yeah,' said Bloat. 'Man against dragon again, just like the good old days.'

'Yeah.'

''Cept you and me wouldn't kill each other, would we?' said Bloat.

'Oh no, not you and me, but all the other humans and dragons would start fighting each other again,' said Brat. 'You and me could have like a little treaty just for us that no one else knows about.'

'Can I have one?' said Scraper.

'What?'

'A little treatie, chocolate one.'

'SHUT UP.'

'So where are your headquarters and your rebel army and all your weapons?' said Bloat. 'I mean, when's it all going to happen?'

'This is the headquarters. Here,' said Brat.

'And the army?'

'We're still recruiting.'

'Weapons?'

'Look at all these rocks,' said Brat. 'They're my secret weapon.'

'Secret?'

'Yes, because the enemy won't realise they're weapons,' said Brat. 'They'll think they're just rocks.'

'They are just rocks,' said Bloat.

'I know. Brilliant, isn't it?' said Brat. 'And I've got a pointy stick.'

In the end Brat was forced to admit that his pointy stick, which wasn't actually pointy because he didn't have anything to sharpen it with, was not so much a weapon as a walking stick he had used to help himself climb up to the cave. He explained that the revolution hadn't actually started and that the only act of rebellion he had done was running away, which had probably made the Cook very cross, but not bothered anyone else at all.

'Though if the Cook is angry, it means she'll probably spit in the Royal Soup like she has every other time something has made her cross, which is at least once a day,' said Brat.

20

'Well, it's a start,' said Bloat encouragingly.

'Yeah. I mean, it's early days,' said Brat. 'We only ran away this morning.'

'Well, there you go,' said Bloat. 'A few hours and you've already got a stick.'

'And a brain-dead idiot with a bucket.'

'Well, things can only improve from now on. Can't they?' said Bloat, cheerfully.

And he was cheerful. It was a strange feeling that he hadn't been expecting. Like Brat, he had dreamt of rebellion and had run away. He hadn't really thought much beyond that. He certainly hadn't the faintest idea how he could change things back to how they used to be. In fact, all he had really thought was going to happen was that he would go up to the cave and hide there for a bit until he got hungry and his parents started to worry and then he'd go home again and pretend to his little brothers and sisters that he been away on a big secret mission. But now he had an ally who was a real rebel, so he could go on real secret missions.

'Don't suppose you brought any spare food with you, did you?' he asked Brat.

21

'No, sorry. I've just got a bag of gristle and a bag of oats for Scraper,' said Brat.

'Oh. It's just that I'm getting a bit hungry,' said Bloat and hurriedly added when he saw the two boys start to look anxious, 'Don't worry, I'm not going to eat you. We're allies, remember?'

'Yeah,' said Brat nervously.

'My mum says all lies are bad,' said Scraper. 'She says you have to tell the troof.'

'SHUT UP.'

'Well, you can have some of my gristle and then I reckon we should go down to the main road and do some highwayman stuff and get some money and food off people,' said Brat. 'And you can breathe fire at them if they won't hand it over.'

Bloat was excited and scared at the same time. His parents had told him that he wasn't allowed to breathe fire at people, not since the treaty with the humans, so the most exciting things he had set fire to had been a clump of grass, a cockroach and his left foot. Not exactly thrilling, though it had brought tears to his eyes. It was obvious that fire-breathing took practice, unless you wanted to keep burning your feet.

So the two incompetent rebels and their even more incompetent assistant went down to the bottom of the valley. Keeping themselves as well hidden as possible, they walked round the edge of Camelot's vast lake until they reached the road and hid behind a big oak tree. Several carriages went by before they summoned up enough courage to leap out and hold one up.

'STOP!' shouted Brat, waving his stick. 'Your money or your life.'

'My life, my life?' said the coachman from his seat high up on the front of the carriage. 'Whatcha going to do? Poke me with your stick?'

'Yeah,' shouted Brat, 'the pointy end.'

'It hasn't got a pointy end,' said the coachman. 'And besides, I've got a gun.'

'Umm, oh,' said Brat, almost but not quite wetting himself. 'Well, er, well, I've got a dragon.'

At which Bloat leapt out from behind the tree, blowing flames. The bag of hay tied to the horse's bridle caught fire.

'Ooh, I'm really scared now,' said the coachman. 'Burning grass.'

'Well, I've got another weapon,' said Brat.

'Oh yeah, what's that then, a catapult?'

'No, a big strong moron,' said Brat as Scraper came out from behind the tree.

As Scraper lumbered towards them, he tripped over a discarded turnip and went crashing into the coach, totally demolishing one of the back wheels. The coach teetered and then the whole thing went crashing over on its side. The coachman's gun was thrown out of his hand and, by a wonderful piece of luck, was thrown into Brat's hand.

'OK,' said Brat. 'Like I said, your money or your life.'

There were three passengers inside the coach and luckily none of them had guns, but they did have quite a lot of money and jewellery and a very big sack of delicious pig's trotters and cabbages. They threw everything out and Scraper collected it all up while Bloat marched up and down blowing flames.

'Why would you want my wife?' said one of the passengers, who was rather deaf.

'What?' said Brat.

'You said your money or your wife,' said the passenger.

'No. I said your ...' Brat began, but the passenger's wife ran across and put her hand over his mouth.

'Don't say a word,' she whispered. 'I've been waiting for an opportunity like this for years.'

'Oh, oh,' she shouted, raising her hands in the air. 'Help, help, I am being abducted. What do you mean, you'll kill me if I don't help you tie everyone up?'

Brat stood open-mouthed as the woman took the rope that had been holding the luggage on top of the coach and tied up the coachman and other passengers. When she'd blindfolded them, she took Brat aside.

'I am the Lady Monaco d'Asparagus,' she said. 'If you ever need somewhere to hide, come to me at the Castle Asparagus.'

'Oh, oh, woe is me,' she shouted. 'How could you be so cruel to a lady as to take me away into this deep dark forest?' And she slipped away into the trees.

Just as the highwaymen were about to follow her into the forest, a troop of soldiers came round the bend. Hearing the approaching horses, the coachman began shouting and the soldiers galloped towards the robbers at top speed.

'Quick,' shouted Brat, scrambling on to the

young dragon's back. 'Quick, Bloat, fly us out of here.'

A small dragon carrying a boy, a big idiot and a sack full of food and money does not soar into the sky like an eagle. Bloat lumbered down the road, flapping his wings like mad, but just could not get off the ground.

'Come on, flap harder,' Brat cried, but it was no good.

Brat grabbed the sack and gave Scraper a kick so he fell off onto the road. That, and the sound of bullets whistling around their heads, was the extra impetus Bloat needed. He soared up into the air and away over the trees.

'What about Scraper?' he said when they reached the cave.

'Plenty more where he came from,' said Brat. 'And look, we've got a gun, some gold and jewels and a lovely bag of food. Pretty good for a first attempt, I reckon.'

'Maybe, and this is only a thought,' said Bloat, 'maybe we should kind of forget about the rebellion and just be highwaymen.'

'We could, couldn't we?' said Brat. 'I mean,

robbing from the citizens of Avalon is rebellion anyway, isn't it?'

'Yeah.'

'And that crazy lady who ran away has given me an idea,' said Brat. 'I think next time we should actually kidnap someone and hold them for ransom. That will really annoy everyone.'

'Yeah, and we could roast them and send them back in a food hamper,' said Bloat.

'No, no. We collect lots of money for not roasting them. That's the point. We threaten to roast them, but we don't actually do it.'

'Not even a little bit?' said Bloat.

'No,' said Brat. 'Unless, of course, they won't pay us.'

The King who was NOT the King who became King when the old King died is not the King any more. Long Live the King.

Meanwhile, apart from the Cook, no one had noticed that Brat had done a runner and if they had, no one would so much have missed him as they were happy to see the back of him. The Cook, of course, was furious, but with the incredible amount of extra work preparing for the coronation, she had no time to try to find the boy.

No one at all noticed that Scraper had gone. He had cleaned the fingernails of the Sewer Cleaners while they were asleep and they had been completely unaware he was doing it. Even when their fingers became infected and began falling off, they still didn't realise someone had been giving them a manicure every night. They just put it down to vicious bacteria.

'Must be all the curries everyone's eating,' the Sewer Cleaners said as they literally worked their fingers to the bone.

Upstairs in the daylight, a wonderful atmosphere of holiday happiness filled the castle. It was like Christmas Day, only all the time and not in a cold place, but somewhere warm like Australia where Christmas is very weird because it's the middle of summer. Five hundred peasants from the surrounding villages had made lovely decorations that were strung all over the castle from the highest towers. No expense had been spared and most of the children were now bald because their hair had been woven into a huge banner welcoming everyone, except all the peasants and their bald children, to the coronation and great party.

The peasants were not, however, being totally left out. On the top of each castle tower, a signaller stood with two flags and as events unfolded inside the castle the signallers spelt it out in semaphore.[4] Semaphore is very slow at the best of times, even more so when the peasants watching the flags can't read or spell. Most villages had a team of twenty-six peasants, each one knowing one letter of the alphabet. This meant that while time moved at its normal speed inside the castle, for those outside it was like a very, very, slow motion action replay. Here is an example:

---

[4] *Of course, this was many centuries before television, when great events can be seen all round the world while they are actually happening. Semaphore is a very slow but effective way of sending messages a long way. A person holds a flag in each hand and the angle they hold the flags symbolises a different letter of the alphabet.*

10am – Friday – King Arthur and his procession come out into the central courtyard of the castle.

10.05am – Friday – The signallers on the towers report this with their flags.

4pm – Friday – The peasants reading the flag messages know there is a King and his name is Art . . .

5pm – Friday – hur.

Then it got dark, so no one could see the flags until someone had the bright idea of setting them alight.

7pm – Friday – The peasants now know that as well as there being a King called Arthur, the signallers are being treated in the sick bay for burns.

The week before the coronation, Camelot had been testing carrier pigeons to tell everyone what was going on and it had been a popular idea with the peasants, who marvelled at the King's kindness in sending them dinners that not only had a little paper napkin tied to their legs, but actually flew into the peasants' houses and waited to be killed. Then they had tried carrier snails, which were a bit slow but also tasted delicious when they arrived six months after the coronation.

'It be wonderful to feel such a part of everything,' said many peasants. 'To know that our wonderful King do want all us humble folks to be part of his corosomething.'

It didn't bother them that by the time they found out their beloved King had actually been crowned, all the leaves had fallen off the trees and there was snow on the ground. They felt the King cared and that was what mattered. Standing outside the castle looking up at the deserted towers for three months and losing several fingers and toes to frostbite was a small price to pay for being a part of the new countrywide harmony that was sweeping Avalon.

Just let any of them foreigners try and invade now, the peasants thought, *and they'll have us to deal with.*

The preparations for the great coronation went without a hitch. King Arthur's new best friends, the dragons, were dressed in finest silk and gold braid by the castle's costumiers. Strutting up and down in front of a big mirror looking magnificent quickly made Spikeweed and Primrose, King and Queen of the Dragons, forget any doubts they might have had about signing a peace treaty with humans.

32

'This is the finest costume I have ever owned,' said Spikeweed. 'Something truly worthy of my Kingness.'

'I think,' said Primrose, 'it's the only costume you've ever owned unless you count the dead grass that used to get stuck in your ears.'

'That wasn't a costume,' said Spikeweed. 'It was an infestation. You know I always had a mouse problem.'

'Anyway, you do look mighty handsome,' said Primrose.

'It's a pity our eldest isn't here,' said Spikeweed.

'Yes. I hope he's not getting into any mischief,' said Primrose. 'You know what a headstrong boy he is.'

'Yes, but I doubt he's off starting a revolution or anything ridiculous like that,' said Spikeweed.

For two days the two dragons flew back and forth carrying visiting dignitaries into the castle for the celebrations. As there were only two dragons, only the most important visitors were flown in.[5] The not-quite-so-important visitors were taken across the lake by boat while everyone else had to ride over the line of bridges and islands.

---

[5] *I.e. the ones most likely to try to invade Camelot.*

Meanwhile, upstairs King Arthur himself was going through the long process of getting ready to be crowned. He would have been quite happy to wear his everyday tights and shirts, but fancy tunic after fancy tunic and tights in every shade of mauve and purple were laid out before him, all clothes that Brat, the Pretender, had adored, but which the true King, who had grown up as a simple peasant who had heard of shoes but wasn't sure they really existed, found garish and decadent.

'Do I have to?' said Arthur. 'They're all really flash and horrible.'

'But you are the King, sire,' said Sir Lancelot, who had been chosen to advise the young monarch on account of his extreme handsomeness and excellent taste in clothes. 'It is expected of you.'

'But, they are awful and anyway,' said Arthur, 'wouldn't it be better if I didn't look exactly the same as the Pretender?'

'True,' said Lancelot. 'And to be perfectly honest, all this stuff is seriously tacky.'

'Yes, it is, good sir knight. So what do you suggest?'

'Well . . .' Lancelot began.

'Could I not wear something like you've got?' Arthur suggested. 'You know, a nice floppy white shirt and some tasteful skin-tight black leather trousers.'

'Indeed, sire,' said Lancelot. 'I always say nothing says good taste on a man better than a pair of shiny leather pants finely crafted from the delicately tanned hide of the archaeopteryx and hand sewn by Giuseppe Armandlegmani Pantalon of Medina. If my liege would permit, I will measure your inside leg this very moment and send instructions by carrier pigeon to Medina this very afternoon.'

'And the shirts?' said King Arthur.

'I have heard from my lady Morgan le Fey that her lady-in-waiting sews the finest thread she has ever seen,' said Lancelot.

'The Lady Petaluna?' said King Arthur as casually as he could.

'Indeed, sire, a sweet young thing, only surpassed

in beauty by her mistress,' said Lancelot as casually as he could.

The thought of Lady Petaluna making him a shirt sent the young King into several states at the same time. The first state was panic at the idea of someone as lovely as Petaluna pressing a tape-measure up against him. The second state was excitement at the idea of someone as lovely as Petaluna pressing a tape-measure up against him. The third state was embarrassment at the idea of someone as lovely as Petaluna pressing a tape-measure up against him.

When he had been the humble kitchen boy, Romeo Crick, and had first set eyes on Morgan le Fey's beautiful lady-in-waiting, Arthur had become very depressed. How could a mere oven-scraper ever hope to win the heart or even little finger of such a high-born lady? Now, though, he was the high-born one, quite a lot higher than the Lady Petaluna in fact. Now, there would be an endless line of desperate mothers introducing their daughters to him in the hope he would marry them and make them Queen. But the King knew in his heart that Lady Petaluna was his one true love.

When word was sent for Lady Petaluna to come and make the King a beautiful shirt for his coronation, the thought of it sent the young girl into several states at the same time. The first state was panic at the thought of pressing a tape-measure up against someone as handsome and perfect and wonderful and unattainable as King Arthur. The second state was excitement at the thought of not so much as pressing a tape-measure up against someone as handsome and perfect and wonderful an unattainable as King Arthur, but of even being in the same room with him when he might not be wearing a shirt.

When she had first set eyes on the King he had been the humble kitchen boy, Romeo Crick, and she had become very depressed. How would she ever be allowed to have a relationship with a mere oven-scraper, when she was such a high-born lady? Now, of course, he was far higher born that she was, so how could she ever hope to compete with the inevitable endless line of desperate mothers introducing their daughters to him in the hope he would marry them and make them Queen? She may have been a lady, but she was only a class-C lady with no wealth, not a true eldest-daughter-Princess-type class-A lady whose very undies would be made with thread of pure gold. After all, her own mother had been only too happy to sell her to Morgan le Fey for a few coins and a set of tea towels depicting pictures of the Lizards, Frogs and Other Amphibians of Camelot.

To add to both of their problems, both King Arthur and Lady Petaluna were extremely, incredibly, painfully shy.

The shirt did not turn out well. It was not because Lady Petaluna couldn't sew very well. She was the finest seamstress in the whole of Avalon. The problem was that because she was so shy she had kept her eyes shut all the time she had been measuring the King. Luckily, Morgan le Fey had given Lady Petaluna a maid of her own the week before, a young girl called Dave.[6] Dave had read the measurements off the tape measure and written them down. Unfortunately Dave was too shy to admit she couldn't read and had just made up the numbers. She couldn't count either, so the numbers were even more inaccurate. Nor

---

[6] *Dave's parents and doctor had been very shy too and had all kept their eyes shut and not realised that Dave was a girl.*

38

could she write so the piece of paper with the King's measurement on was not so much a list of detailed figures as a lot of scribbles.[7]

Lady Petaluna was too embarrassed to admit she had kept her eyes shut and too embarrassed to admit that she couldn't read either, so she had made the shirt by guesswork, but love is blind so King Arthur thought the shirt was wonderful.

'Isn't it wonderful,' he said to Lancelot. 'And it fits me like a glove.'

'Indeed, your majesty, but for whose hand?'

Because Arthur was King no one else dared say it was dreadful. In fact, within two hours there were people wearing exact copies.

'I think it is brilliant,' said a Yuppie To The Court of King Arthur. 'I cannot imagine why no one has ever thought of making one sleeve twice as long as the other before.'

'Yes, and three sleeves, too,' said another. 'So clever for those embarrassing times when you lose a

---

[7] *Interestingly, Dave's scribbles were very lovely to look at and within five years were selling for up to ten groats a dozen at Avalon's only art gallery – SoThyBuys.*

sleeve or dip your cuff in your soup.'

'Which, with one sleeve so long, happens frequently,' said a third.

But poor Lady Petaluna knew the shirt was a disaster and lay on her bed in tears. Any slight hopes she might have had of the King falling in love with her were gone forever.

If only there was a wise book called the Blue Sages *or maybe the* Yellow Sages *that listed different types of places throughout the land that one might wish to go,* she thought, *I would find me a remote monastery and hie me there to spend the rest of my life as a nun wearing naught but sackcloth and eating ashes and gruel for every meal, even Christmas dinner.*

O woe is me, she thought too.

I are totally full of woe, she added.

'But my lady,' said Dave, 'the King thinks your shirt most wonderful.'

'He can't do,' Petaluna sobbed. 'He's just saying it to be kind.'

'Indeed, my lady, he says it to spare your feelings,' said Dave.

'Oh, I hadn't thought of that.'

40

'And wouldst thou not wish him to be kind to thee?'

'More than anything in the whole world,' said Petaluna.

'Well, my lady, your wish is granted,' said Dave.

Petaluna fainted.

The Coronation

The day of the coronation finally arrived and everything was ready. Visitors had arrived from many lands, some coming by dragon, some by balloon, others by road or river or sea, a few by flying carpet or enchanted pumpkin. Two princes even arrived by parcel post. The whole world saw the coronation as the first day of a new and exciting era, more new and exciting than any new and exciting era had ever been before.

Probably the least excited person was the young King himself. He was a modest boy and until recently had lived a simple uncomplicated life. Apart from being carried off as a newborn baby and rescued by two poor but honest peasants who had raised him as their own and then got killed leaving him alone with a pig called Geoffrey who had been struck by lightning leaving him alone with nothing but a very tasty dinner of pork and then being stuffed into a sack and sold to the Cook at Camelot who had discovered that he was fireproof, the boy had led an uneventful life. After all, being carried off and ending up in a sack with the taste of roast pork in your mouth was the sort of thing that happened to young children all the time in those days.

'Do we have to have all this fuss?' he kept asking Sir Lancelot.

'Oh my lord, I know exactly how you feel and I do sympathise,' said Sir Lancelot, 'but it is tradition and that is what life is all about. It is your royal duty.'

'I suppose so,' said Arthur, 'but I'd as soon have a cup of tea and a bun and just let everyone assume I was the King without all this pomp and ceremony.'

'I know, my lord, but think of the positive things,' said Sir Lancelot. 'Tell me if I am wrong, but I think you are quite sweet on my wonderful lady Morgan le Fey's lady-in-waiting, Lady Petaluna, are you not?'

'I am,' said the King, 'but please, good knight, promise you will tell no one.'

'Of course not, sire.'

'And I, in turn, will tell no one that you are in love with my sister.'

'I, what? Oh umm,' Sir Lancelot stammered and fainted.

When he came to, he fell to his knees before the young King and begged forgiveness.

'What for?' said Arthur.

44

'Well, my lord, the incredibly wonderful and divine and gorgeous and magnificent Lady Morgan le Fey is far above me,' said Sir Lancelot. 'She is, after all, the daughter of a King and the sister of a King and I am but a humble knight. With your permission, sire, I will take me to the highest tower of Camelot and throw myself off onto the sharp rocks below that the vampires may come and devour my worthless remains.'

'Oh, don't be silly,' said Arthur. 'This is not the Dark Ages. These are the Days of Yore – no one throws themselves off high towers any more. They simply take poison.'

'Very well, sire. I shall take me to the chemist this very hour.'

'Only joking,' said the King. 'You will do such thing. I may be only a child, but I'm pretty sure my sister is pretty keen on you too.'

'I cannot believe that, my lord,' said Sir Lancelot, who was used to women falling at his feet wherever he went, but still couldn't believe the wonderful Morgan le Fey could care for him.

'Believe it or not,' said King Arthur, 'I totally

45

forbid you to kill yourself in any way at all and if you do, you will be punished.'

'But sire, if I am dead, how could I be punished more?'

'You will be brought back to life and killed in a really messy and painful way,' said the King. 'Now forget about all that and help me get ready, please.'

'Indeed, sire,' said Sir Lancelot without the slightest hint of sarcasm. 'I am your majesty's most devoted servant.'

He really did mean it. He could sense greatness in this slight young boy standing before him. When he had first met Arthur, he had thought him so shy and uneducated that he would probably not survive long enough to make his coronation. There were any number of potential assassins in the world and the boy seemed like a sitting duck – not just a duck that was sitting there looking around at the world, but a duck that was sitting there fast asleep in a big ovenproof dish – but now there was a new air of kingliness about him.

Arthur could sense this kingliness creeping into his soul. The timid child he had always been was being replaced by a new, stronger personality that

would eventually make him the greatest ruler who had ever lived, and he had Sir Lancelot to thank for the transformation. A few months earlier, the boy would have slipped into the shadows and kept silent, but now, by ordering the greatest knight in the world to not kill himself and having the greatest knight in the world obeying him, he realised he had true power, not just the power of being the King, but a great power that had been asleep inside him since he had been born.

When he had first been told he was the true King, Arthur hadn't really believed it. Sure, he had the Mark of the King on his back to prove it, but part of him had wondered if it wasn't just a coincidence, maybe a bruise or something. But now he knew in his heart that he really was the one true King of Avalon, even if he didn't like purple tights, and he felt as if he had suddenly grown two feet taller.[8]

The boy and the knight felt a strong bond unite them. It was an unspoken bond because men don't talk about that sort of thing, but it was there and they both

---

[8] *Since he had been told he was the true King, Arthur had actually grown two millimetres taller, but then so had every other child of his age.*

knew it. Now he was ready for his coronation.

As Sir Lancelot led the young King out into the vast courtyard in the centre of Camelot, Merlin saw instantly the change that had come over the boy. Even in his three-armed disaster of a shirt, he walked with a regal air he had not had a few hours earlier. It had been Merlin who had appointed Sir Lancelot to take the boy under his wing and the old wizard knew he had made the right choice.

The Days of Yore would go down in history as the Days of Yore and be remembered as the time when Avalon achieved a greatness it had only dreamt of until now.

All will be well in the world, Merlin thought. *Though of course, having achieved its ultimate greatness, where is there to go but down?*

But Merlin was like that. He always saw the worst-case scenario. In his eyes the glass was less than half full and there were dirty brown things floating in it.

'I am not a pessimist,' he would say when people told him he was a pessimist. 'I am a realist. I just like to be prepared for every possible situation.'

Which of course he wasn't, otherwise he would

know that Princess Floridian was determined to find Excalibur and take over the world.[9]

The Great Throne of Kings was the biggest chair that had ever been made. In the Dark Ages the Kings had been great big lumpy people. That was how they had become King, by sitting on all their enemies until they were overcome with dead. But over the last few generations, in the sort of grey space between the Dark Ages ending and the Days of Yore beginning, the Kings had got smaller. They had stopped sitting on people, except for fun that is, and gone over to the hereditary system where the new King did not have to be stronger or cleverer or have any qualifications at all to become King.[10] All he had to do now was be the son of the existing King.

---

[9] *Not only was King Arthur unprepared, but so are you because you don't know about Princess Floridian either. It's all right, though, because she will be along shortly.*

[10] *A system still widely used today.*

Being a skinny boy of eleven, King Arthur couldn't actually climb up onto the throne so there was a short delay while a peasant was fetched, scrubbed down and made to lie on the ground in front of the throne. Arthur still couldn't reach and it took a pile of seven peasants neatly piled up to form a small staircase before he could finally clamber up onto the big red cushion.

It hadn't just been the Kings who had got smaller. So had everyone else. By the time they had set everything up so the Archbishop and his two assistants and the Lord Chamberlain were in place, there was a pile of forty-two peasants scattered around the throne. There had been frantic begging and arm-waving when volunteers had been called for to form the human stage. It wasn't just the luxury of being scrubbed down, a luxury most peasants could only dream of, or the promise of three potatoes every single week forever,[11] but the honour of serving their new King in such a proud and noble way.

As the crowd looked on in awed silence, the

---

[11] *There are still three families of English aristocrats who claim their three potatoes a week to this very day.*

50

Archbishop took the Great Crown of Avalon and placed it on Arthur's head. Being so small, the crown not only fell right past his head, it actually slipped down over his shoulders, pinning his arms to his sides. Two handmaidens were called to stand behind the new King, holding up the crown so it looked like it was sitting in the right place.

'Blah, blah, blah, yea, verily blah, blah, blah,' droned the Archbishop.

No one was actually listening to a single word he was saying, but every time he paused for breath, the crowd let out a great cheer.

'Blah, blah, blah, pronounce you King,' the Archbishop said and fell to his knees to kiss the King's hand.

'Great,' said Arthur. 'Can we start the party now?'

'Yes, please,' whimpered the two handmaidens, whose arms were burning with pain.

Arthur stood up, the peasants rearranged themselves and he climbed down to the ground.

Party on Ye Dudes

King Arthur and all his top guests sat in a semicircle eating pleasant pheasant sandwiches and Special Royal Ginger Beer while a string of entertainers entertained them. First off was –

MALMSLEY COHEN[12]
Court Jester
A Joke, A Song & Some Bacon

'I say, I say, I say, a very funny thing happened to me on my way here today,' said the Jester. 'No seriously, it did. We was coming here on the Chelmsford Stage when we was held up by highwaymen. No, hold on. I'll start again. I say, I say, I say, a very scary thing happened to me on my way here today, No, no, don't laugh.'

No one did.

'Well, I say highwaymen, but really they was highway children, a weedy little boy and a weedy little dragon. No, missus, I kid you not. And they had, wait for it, they had a big lumbering potato with them

---

[12] *Malmsley Cohen was my great-grandfather and I've been told he was the family clown.*

53

who upturned the stagecoach and robbed us. Put all our valuables in a bucket and made off with them. Actually, now I think back, it wasn't very funny thing at all. It was really scary and I was really frightened. No, I mean, don't laugh.'

Everyone did.

'No, no,' said Malmsley as the post-traumatic shock began to take effect. 'Don't laugh.'

Everyone laughed and then they stopped, took big swigs of ginger beer and threw pleasant pheasant sandwich crusts at the sad figure of the Court Jester who was now weeping and shaking uncontrollably.

Then they laughed a lot more.

Malmsley fell down and curled up into a sobbing, shivering ball on the floor.

Everyone laughed and laughed, took a deep breath and laughed some more. Then they began throwing money.

'No, I mean, no, oops, oh dear,' cried Malmsley, wetting himself.

More laughter followed by lots and lots of money, so much money that soon the jester was buried in it.

Ooo-er, Malmsley, old chap, that went down well, he thought, *and who would have thought a huge pile of cash could lifts one's spirits so and actually cure post-traumatic shock.*

He got to his feet and took a great bow which brought loud cheers and even more money. At the end of the day, all the money thrown at him plus his performing fee minus the tiny bit of cash the highwaymen had stolen meant he was now quite rich and had had three offers of marriage. Considering the trouble he'd been having paying his rent, Malmsley Cohen was a happy man. Over the ensuing years he would incorporate the sobbing and falling over into his act, until he ended up very rich and happily married to three beautiful women who were even richer.[13]

'This young dragon,' said Spikeweed, taking Malmsley to one side, 'you didn't happen to catch his

---

[13] *It was the law in those days that Court Jesters were allowed to have as many as seven wives, though none of them were allowed to be sheep. This had bothered Malmsley when he was poor, as the only living thing who ever smiled at him was actually a rather attractive sheep called Felicity. When he became rich a lot of people who were not sheep started smiling at him. Yet more evidence that money can buy you love and happiness.*

name, did you?'

'I did indeed, sir,' said the jester.

'Well, good sir, if you will tell me the name,' said Spikeweed, knowing what the answer would be, 'I will be happy to fly you and your money safely back to your home.'

'Bloat,' said Malmsley. 'The boy called him Bloat.'

'And the boy's name,' said Morgan le Fey, who had been listening to the conversation. 'I don't suppose you got that, did you?'

'I did indeed, my lady,' said Malmsley, 'though I say I did, but it could just be what the young dragon called him. I mean, Brat isn't a real name, is it?'

'Oh yes it is,' said Morgan le Fey. 'It is indeed.'

The second act was –

ARMOIRE
The Donkey Lifter

Armoire was built like a small castle, not a tall elegant castle with pointy spires, but a square block with narrow slit windows and one very small door. While his assistants set up his equipment, Armoire strangled

five sets of bagpipes with his bare hands.

Once everything was set, Armoire climbed up a wobbly bamboo tower until he was standing one hundred feet above a very sharp, pointy rock that had been placed directly beneath him. Then a beautiful assistant climbed the tower to blindfold him while two male assistants followed her up carrying four donkeys.

When all was ready, Armoire walked out to the end of a narrow plank, caught the four donkeys and began to juggle them.

Even though the dragons had made a peace treaty with the humans, there were a few distant dragon cousins who had come to Avalon for the coronation, who thought life had become quite dull now they were not setting fire to things and attacking Noble Knights. Two of these young dragons were hiding on the roof of a tall tower and as Armoire began to juggle, they began to blow. There were no flames, just big gusts of hot wind and these big gusts of hot wind were aimed right at Armoire's bamboo tower.

The whole structure began to move, very slightly at first, but as the dragons blew harder, it gathered momentum until it was swaying backwards and

forwards like the pendulum of a big clock. Some of the knots holding the whole thing together became untied and gradually all the string began to unravel.

Armoire's three assistants scrambled back down to the ground as the entire structure began to come to bits. Everyone, including the King and his party, fled as bamboo began to rain down round them.

The donkeys looked terrified, not the normal everyday-looking terrified that being juggled a hundred feet up in the air brings, but the special kind of terrified brought by the realisation that they were probably all about to become very flat rugs on the rocks below.

Being blindfolded, Armoire didn't realise any of this was happening. Of course, he could feel the tower swaying backward and forwards, but he though it was just happening inside his head and tummy because of the powerful curried archaeopteryx he had eaten for dinner the night before. All he knew was that he couldn't hear anyone cheering, because they had run away out of earshot, and it made him very upset.

I'll show them, he thought, and in the split second when all four donkeys were in the air, he began to do a strip tease while singing the Belgian National Anthem

in such a deep booming voice that it made the entire bamboo scaffold vibrate as well as sway violently at exactly the right pitch to make all the remaining bits of string come untied.

'I think I can say, without fear of contradiction,' said Merlin as everyone peered out of the castle windows to see what was going to happen, 'I think I can say, it will end in tears.'

Unbelievably, it didn't.

The wind gave one almighty gust and the whole construction – the bamboo, the string, Armoire with his trousers half off and the four donkeys – was lifted into the air, carried over the castle walls and dumped into the lake.

And yet there was even more to come. As the bamboo and string fell towards the lake the wind whipped it up and down and threw it around until it all wove itself into an unsinkable raft with Armoire and three of the donkeys in the middle of it.[14]

---

[14] *Where the fourth donkey ended up will be revealed later, but be reassured it was not eaten by an olm. All four actually ended up in the same place, but the fourth one took a short cut and got there before the others.*

The applause was staggering, probably the loudest noise ever heard anywhere in the whole world. A boat was dispatched to tow the raft ashore. Before the boat reached them, the three donkeys panicked and threw themselves into the water. Armoire, who still had his blindfold on, hadn't the faintest idea what had happened, but the applause told him it must have gone fairly well. When his beautiful assistant told him what *had* happened, he fainted.

'That is the most amazing act I have ever seen in my life,' said King Arthur when Armoire regained consciousness.

This didn't really mean much, because up until then the only act he had ever seen had been Malmsley Cohen.

'I hereby dub thee Lord Armoire Of The Scaffolding and grant you seventeen acres of freehold land, five potatoes a week and a quart of ale every fortnight.'

Anything that followed Armoire's act was bound to be an anti-climax. The fire-eaters ate not just their fire, but the entire pizza oven down the last brick, and barely raised a cheer.

Even –

failed to excite the audience. The show's high point, a life-size model of Athene the Goddess of Love made entirely out of the finest cheddar cheese, totally failed to excite them. Even when a huge flock of magpies swooped down and ate it they were bored. All they could think of was the amazing Armoire and his donkeys flying through the air towards the lake. Only when the magpies, smelling cheese on the Myth Buskers' fingers, actually pecked them to death and ate them did they show any signs of interest.

'That was a bit violent,' said a visiting Queen, but it was the Days of Yore, when being pecked to death by cheese-crazed animals happened all the time.

'You should have been around in the Dark Ages,' said her husband, King Mozzarella. 'We had exploding cheese in those days. Everyone got covered in it. It was wonderful except for the bits of Myth Busker that kept getting caught in your teeth.'

After the Ball was (bounced) Over

As the festivities were drawing to a close and most of the guests were wending[15] their way back across the bridges to the mainland, an old man came staggering through the castle into the courtyard, where he collapsed. His clothes were torn and covered in blood and the hem of his coat was smouldering as if it had been recently set on fire. The crowd parted as Merlin went over to the man.

'Tell me, old man,' said the wizard, 'how dare you come to our great King's coronation in such a disgusting state?'

'I am not as I look,' said the old man. 'I am King Kasterwheel of Westerland come to join in the celebrations and honour King Arthur.'

'But what had happened to you, my poor man?' said King Arthur.

'We was robbed,' he said. 'Set upon by highwaymen and all our worldly goods was taken from us.'

'These highwaymen . . .' Morgan le Fey began.

---

[15] *Wending was extremely popular in the Days of Yore. Now we have GPS no one 'wends' anymore. We simply 'go'.*

'Not so much men as children, my lady,' said King Kasterwheel.

'A boy and a dragon?'

'Indeed so, and a big walking potato all covered in cuts and bruises,' said the King. 'They took all my money and the great ruby I was bringing as a gift to the King and they took my most treasured and beautiful possession, my daughter the Princess Floridian.'

'Who, I have no doubt,' said Merlin, 'they mean to hold for ransom.'

'Indeed, sir. I have already received a note that the dastardly fiends forced my beloved daughter to write. It was brought to me by carrier pigeon as I crawled here.'

While a servant took the old man away to get his wounds seen to and fit him out with new clothes, Morgan le Fey and Merlin made plans.

'When they make the arrangements to collect the ransom,' said Merlin, 'we shall be ready for them. No mere boy and baby dragon shall get the better of us.'

'You know who this boy is, don't you?' said Morgan le Fey.

'No.'

'It is the vile child who pretended to be the King,' said Morgan le Fey. 'The Cook tells me he ran away a few days ago. As you know, he is a crafty, evil child.'

'Indeed he is, but I think he is no match for us,' said Merlin. 'Methinks it will not be too hard to capture him.'

Me also thinks, thought Merlin, *that rescuing the Princess Floridian should bring a nice reward.*

'No doubt, you'll be thinking of the handsome reward for rescuing the Princess?' said Morgan le Fey.

'It never crossed my mind, your highness,' said Merlin. 'Though I must admit it is a very beautiful idea.'

'I don't imagine it did cross your mind, my friend,' Morgan le Fey said with a smile. 'I imagine it entered your mind and stayed there.'

'Handsome reward?' said Sir Bedivere, the famous Mercenary Knight who had sold his own mother eleven times.[16] 'When we do we start?'

'We are not here to discuss the reward,' said Morgan le Fey, who had far more money than she

---

[16] *He had trained her well, so like a good homing pigeon Sir Bedivere's mother kept finding her way home again.*

would ever need. 'We are here to make plans to rescue the Princess Floridian, who I have no doubt has golden hair around an angelic face of porcelain beauty and two large blue eyes filled with sweet innocence and trust and a beautiful rosebud mouth that has never kissed another, as all traditional kidnapped princesses do.'

King Kasterwheel, returned with his wounds washed and wearing a borrowed dressing gown, hung his head and nodded.

'She is as you say, my lady, a precious jewel next to which all other jewels appear as dull pieces of glass,' said the King. 'Yourself excepted, of course, my lady.'

'Fear not, my friend,' said Morgan le Fey. 'Our noble knights shall rescue your daughter and restore her to your safekeeping.'

'I thank you, my lady,' said the King. 'I don't suppose there's any food left from the great banquet, is there? Bit of venison or swan, or even a rat's leg. No food has passed my mouth since early this morning.'

'Oh, sire, what were we thinking? A servant shall take you to the kitchen for a partridge burger and chippies while we make plans to rescue your beloved child.'

'Thank you, your highness, your kindness will not go unrewarded.'

Ooh, I like the sound of that, thought Merlin and Sir Bedivere unanimously. They knew that the visiting King was just about one of the richest Kings in the entire world.

'I think I need to make you aware of the Royal Decree that says any rewards for highwaymen-capturing or hostage-rescuing automatically become the property of the King and will be used to set up an orphanage for destitute baby unicorns,' said Morgan le Fey, who could read minds, particularly men's minds, which she said were as hard to read as a two-year-old's bunny rabbit book. 'That is the tradition.'

'Tradition?' said Merlin. 'Since when?'

'Since about thirty seconds ago,' said Morgan le Fey. 'All traditions have to start somewhere.'

Merlin and Sir Bedivere both looked extremely annoyed, even when Morgan le Fey said there was a good chance that whoever did rescue the Princess would probably be given her hand in marriage, which was another, much older tradition.

I'm too old for a young wife, thought Merlin. *All*

67

that dancing and jousting and carousing, and then she'd probably run off with a younger man and end up with half my fortune.

I do not want the expense of a young wife, thought Sir Bedivere. *All that dancing and jousting and carousing, and then she'd probably run off with a handsome man and end up with half my fortune.*

'Well, my lady, we will leave it for you to sort out a plan,' said Merlin, sliding off towards his private quarters.

'Indeed, though of course, if you need a hand, just give us a call,' said Sir Bedivere, climbing on his horse and galloping away very fast in all directions.

Morgan le Fey sent for Sir Lancelot who, as it has already been stated, adored her in the same way the King adored Lady Petaluna, which was incredibly. He was not as shy as the King. Over the years his noble deeds of legendary bravery in far off, quite near and really a long way away lands had brought him many, many girlfriends of every shape, size, colour and species. He had swept them all off their feet with his dashing good looks, amazing charm, razor-sharp wit and a large broom. He had never been lost for words whatever the language or situation and always knew exactly the right thing to say to win a lady's heart. But now, all that talent had deserted him. In the presence of Morgan le Fey he was as useless as his King. He blushed. He stammered and he knocked his knees together.

'I cannot understand it,' he said to his squire, Grimethorpe, later. 'I have no trouble with women. They fall at my feet like socks.'

'Socks?'

'Not new socks, but old ones that have been washed in water that was too hot so they won't stay up any more and keep falling down inside your boots,' Sir Lancelot explained.

'Ah, those socks, my lord,' said Grimethorpe, 'the ones you kindly give to me.'

'Indeed so.'

'They do indeed, sire, I can vouch for that,' said Grimethorpe. 'When we were abroad in those hot, romantic countries, I was forever tripping over them.'

'What, my socks?'

'No, my lord, all your girlfriends.'

'Absolutely,' said Lancelot. 'So how come I am

so tongue-tied and useless in the presence of my lady Morgan le Fey?'

'I can only think of one reason, my lord.'

'Pray tell. Do you think I have some dreaded ague, some mysterious oriental disease that maketh even the greatest of men as feeble as a puppy?'

'No, my lord.'

'Think you that I may have caught ladybug pox[17] or piglet flu?'[18]

'No, my lord.'

'Not the dreaded Whooping Sneeze.'[19]

'No, my lord.'

'Then I am confused, good squire,' said Sir Lancelot. 'What think you my illness may be?'

'You are in love, my lord.'

'Surely not,' said the brave knight. 'Are you absolutely sure? I thought I had a natural immunity

---

[17] *Which is like chicken pox except the spots are bright purple and much, much smaller and the patient is really embarrassed because they look so silly.*

[18] *See the previous footnote.*

[19] *Like whooping cough, but with a lot more, and I mean a lot more, mess.*

70

to all that sort of thing.'

'No one is immune to love, my lord, apart from politicians and geography teachers and the entire population of Germany,' said Grimethorpe.

'Well, I'm certainly none of those,' said Sir Lancelot. 'Gosh.'

'Indeed, my lord.'

'So what do you think I should do?'

'Well, my lord, this is the Days of Yore,' said Grimethorpe. 'The standard procedure is to Plight your Troth.'

'Absolutely. No problem,' said Sir Lancelot. 'I shall do it this very day. Now, be a good fellow and nip down to the market and get me one.'

'One what, my lord?'

'A Troth,' said Sir Lancelot. 'And make sure you get the very best. Spare no expense. My lady Morgan le Fey deserves only the very finest that money can buy.'

'You don't exactly know what a troth is, do you, my lord?' said Grimethorpe.

'Not exactly, but I'm sure I shall recognise it when you return with one.'

'Let me explain, my lord,' said Grimethorpe. 'You

should probably sit down.'

Grimethorpe sat just out of arm's reach from his master and explained. Sir Lancelot went white, then red, then white again, then a colour that hasn't got a name but is much paler than white.

'So it's not something a horse drinks out of?' he said.

'No, my lord, that is a trough.'

'Or a serving wench with very white skin and black hair?'

'No, my lord, that is a goth.'

'Right, so no need to go down to the market then?'

'Indeed there is, my lord,' said Grimethorpe. 'I think Troth Plighting always works better when accompanied by a bunch of flowers and a nice box of choccies.'

'I see,' said Sir Lancelot. 'So first thing tomorrow or the day after we shall go to the market and procure them.'

'The market is closed tomorrow and the day after, my lord,' said Grimethorpe. 'It is the Feast of Saint Intestine and they are public holidays.'

'Oh dear, so they are.'

'The market is open today, my lord. I shall fetch your horse this very moment,' said Grimethorpe and ran out of the room before Lancelot could say anything.

Sir Lancelot came over all faint and had to lie down. The idea of being in love was as foreign to him as a Belgian recipe for Hungarian Goulash. He had heard the word love before, but then he had heard a lot of words including *dandelion*, *trousers* and *persecute* without understanding what any of them meant.

He knew what love meant. It meant you couldn't talk properly in front of the person you were in love with and you went red all over and got a tummy ache that even a badger pie could not relieve. It meant you didn't know if you were coming or going or about to do neither or both. It meant you put your socks on the wrong feet which made you walk round in circles.

It meant, *oh I don't know what it meant, I mean, means*, Sir Lancelot thought as he lay on the daybed by the window.

Maybe I need a strong cup of tea, he thought, *except that tea is just a rumour and we won't know if it's real for at least two hundred years when a strange man*

called Sir Walter Riley will return from a long sea voyage with a bag of dried leaves that my descendants will be stupid enough to drink when he boils them up in a kettle.

So maybe I'll just have a glass of strong water.

As he lay there in this delirious state, the object of his love knocked softly on the door and came into the room.

'Oh my lord,' said the staggeringly beautiful Morgan le Fey, seeing Lancelot lying there in a swoon, 'are you unwell?'

And before the great knight could reply she sat herself beside him and began mopping his fevered brow with a delicate lace handkerchief dipped in rosewater that she just happened to have been carrying.[20] Of course this made Sir Lancelot swoon even more.

---

[20] *This was not that unusual in those days. Most fine ladies carried a bucket or two of rosewater and a sack full of hankies wherever they went. This was because the Days of Yore were very smelly. I imagine that you are very surprised to learn that biological Spray n' Wipe had not been invented in those days – it was, in fact, invented by William Shakespeare in 1478 at half past three. So fine ladies walked around with rosewater-soaked hankies stuffed up their noses to avoid the terrible stinks that assaulted them from every side.*

74

'Oh my lord,' Morgan le Fey cried. 'What ails you?'

'Gibber, gibber, gibber, mumble.'

'If I may be so bold, my lady,' said Grimethorpe, who had followed Morgan le Fey into the room. 'I can explain. My lord is in love.'

'Surely not,' said Morgan le Fey. 'Sir Lancelot's affairs of the heart are legendary. He is the most handsome man in the whole world. Why, it is said that he falls in love more often than he changes his socks and I am told he changes his socks once a month.'

Sir Lancelot gibbered some more, then mumbled, then opened his mouth over and over again then fainted.

'Now my master is unconscious, my lady, I will take the liberty of explaining,' said Grimethorpe.

He told Morgan le Fey that indeed there was some truth to the rumours, but all the hundreds of women who had fallen at his master's feet had merely been girlfriends. Only now, for the first time in his life, had Sir Lancelot actually fallen in love.

'As you can see, it has taken him unawares and turned him into a gibbering idiot,' said Grimethorpe.

Morgan le Fey, who had also not been in love

before she had met Sir Lancelot, was a girl, so she knew all about all that love stuff and was not swooning. Her heart, however, was beating dangerously fast because she was sure the person Lancelot had fallen in love with could not be her. She began to feel faint.

'I see you are feeling faint, my lady,' said Grimethorpe. 'If I am not mistaken, you too are in love and as someone who has seen more troths plighted than you've had hot dinners, I can tell it is my master who is the object of your heart's desire. Well, let me put you out of your misery, my lady. You are the one my master loves. Were he conscious, he would probably be plighting his troth this very moment.'

Morgan le Fey fainted.

'Ah,' said Grimethorpe. 'Better go and get some more smelling salts.'

MEAL OF THE MONTH

SERF SOUP

With **Fresh Brains**
and at least two Serf's Ears per serving.*
AND
our written guarantee that it contains
NO broccoli or other dangerous vegetables.
AND NOW
with added peanuts, MSG and gluten.
Yum, yum!

* In the event of an ingredients shortage, we reserve the right to replace ears with nostrils.

*This week with
FREE HAIRS!*

Meanwhile, at the Notorious Highwaypersons' Secret Headquarters . . .

'Call this a secret hideout?' said Princess Floridian. 'It's pathetic. And if any one of you pushes me once more or even touches any bit of me with the tiniest tip of your finger, you will be coughing up your kneecaps.'

'Hey, no, I mean, umm,' said Scraper, who had managed against all the odds to find his way back to the cave. 'You are our prisoner. You are not supposed to talk to us like that.'

'Listen, potato boy, you come one step nearer and I'll kick your bucket down the mountain.'

'I don't think so, missy,' said Brat. 'We're in charge. We tell you what to do.'

'Don't be pathetic.'

'We've got a gun,' said Bloat, 'and we're not afraid to use it.'

'Go on then,' said Princess Floridian.

'Well, I can't,' said Bloat. ''Cause I ain't got no thumbs, but our noble leader, the real King Arthur, he could use it.'

'Yeah,' said Brat. 'I'm living on the edge, I am, so don't mess with me.'

'Living on the edge, living on the edge? More like living in a hedge. You're pathetic and everyone knows you are no more the real King than potato boy here.'

'Well, we managed to kidnap you.'

'No you didn't, you pathetic little wimp. I ran away because I thought it would be more fun than going to a boring wedding,' said the Princess.

'Well, you're our prisoner now,' said Bloat.

'No I'm not. I can just walk down to the castle whenever I want.'

'Just you try it,' said Brat.

The Princess stood up and walked out of the cave.

'No, no, listen,' said Bloat. 'I mean, how do you think you'll find your way down then, eh?'

'What, you mean, apart from the fact I can see the castle from here and the footpath with a sign saying "This way to Camelot"?' said Princess Floridian.

'Yeah, well umm . . .' Brat began.

'And,' the Princess continued, 'if this place is so secret and hard to find, how did potato boy find his way back here?'

'I just asked someone,' said Scraper, 'and they showed me the signpost what I followed.'

'Signpost?'

'Yes, the one at the bottom of the path that says "Secret Hideout six hundred metres ahead, first on the left".'

'Do you honestly expect any of us to believe that you can read?' said Princess Floridian.

'No, well, but someone read it to me,' said Scraper.

'Do you honestly expect any of us to believe that you can remember ten words?' said Princess Floridian.

'Are you saying I am stupid?'

'Well, actually, I don't need to. You just did,' said the Princess. 'Now, summing up, you are basically the dumbest highwaymen ever who couldn't hold up your own trousers, never mind a stagecoach, and your secret hideout is about as well hidden as Old Mrs Craftwork's World Famous Tripe & Onions Tearooms, which are the most famous and most visited tearooms in the whole world and ninety-seven per cent of the population know exactly how to get to them.'

'We did hold up a stagecoach,' said Brat, turning red as his trousers fell down, 'and we got a gun and some money and a very big huge shiny red thing.'

'It's a ruby,' said Princess Floridian. 'The one my

father was going to give to King Arthur as a coronation present. You will give it to me now.'

'No,' said Brat. 'It's mine.'

The Princess took hold of Brat's ear and twisted it until he started to cry. He fell to his knees and as he looked up at the Princess she dribbled in his face. She wanted to spit on him, but being a Princess she had to remain dignified and dribbling could always be looked upon as maybe being an accident. Brat handed over the ruby.

'Do you know how much this is worth?' said the Princess.

'Don't care,' said Brat, who was having the biggest sulk he had ever had and he had had mega sulks when he had been King.

'Ten million gold crowns.'

Brat fainted. So did Bloat. Scraper just sat there with his mouth hanging open, which it had been doing ever since the Princess had threatened his beloved bucket.

'I will tell you what we are doing to do,' said the Princess. 'We are going to leave here and find a proper secret hideout that is actually secret and not such a

long hard climb halfway up a mountain and hasn't got stuff that looks like snot running down the walls. Then we are going to get properly organised and do some proper highway robbery, kidnapping, looting and pillaging and make us some serious money.'

'You're not in charge,' Brat snivelled. 'I am. I am the proper King Arthur and I should be the King of Everywhere.'

'Well, that's not going to happen is it, Mister King of Nowhere?' said the Princess. 'So now you've got two choices. You will either do what I say and I will be in charge or I will drag, throw and drop you down this mountain, take you back to Camelot and claim a huge reward. You will be thrown into the deepest dungeon and left there until you die.'

'There's three of us,' said Brat in a last defiant gesture. 'We could easily overpower you.'

Princess Floridian picked up Scraper's bucket and jammed it on the gaping idiot's head. She knocked Bloat onto his back and sat Scraper on the young dragon's wings. Then she picked up Brat and rubbed him up against the wall until he was totally covered in the snotty slime.

'You were saying?' she said.

Brat wasn't saying.

None of them were. Brat and Scraper had both wet their trousers. Bloat didn't have trousers because he was a dragon, so he had just wet his own feet.

They collected their few bits and pieces, including the gun which was actually not a real gun but one carved out of a sheep bone that had been a free gift in a sack of dried gruel, and followed the Princess out of the cave.

As they walked down towards the vast lake surrounding the incredible castle of Camelot, the clouds that had covered the sky all day opened slightly and a narrow beam of brilliant sunlight broke through. It shone like a searchlight onto a small rock in the middle of the lake, where it reflected on something shiny, sending tiny beams of light in all directions.

Princess Floridian stopped and stared.

'Oh my God,' she said. 'Can the rumours be true?'

'Rumours?' said Brat.

'What rumours?' said Bloat.

'I likes rhubarb,' said Scraper.

'SHUT UP,' said everyone else.

'Excalibur,' said the Princess. 'The One True Sword of the King. Even in my country we have heard of it, though we all thought it was a fairy story, though as these are the Days of Yore, you can never tell whether fairy stories are made up or real.'

'Your what?' said Scraper.

'What?'

'Days of your what?' said Scraper.

'Shut up,' said Brat.

'The legend says that whoever can pull Excalibur from the rock is the one true King of Avalon,' said the Princess.

'That's me,' said Brat. 'That's my sword, that is, and I'm going to get it.'

He told the Princess what had happened. How he had been thrown off the throne by his enemies and down to the kitchens.

'I know,' said the Princess.

'What do you mean, you know?' said Brat.

'Everyone knows,' said the Princess. 'Everyone in the whole entire all of the world knows.'

Brat went very silent then said, 'So I suppose

they all feel really sorry for me.'

'Not exactly,' said the Princess.

'Some of them must.'

'I wouldn't count on it.'

'But I used to be totally in charge,' said Brat. 'I had more pairs of tights in more shades of mauve than anyone else in the whole world! And look at me now, stumbling down a muddy track wearing sackcloth breeches that won't even stay up. Come on, we'll get a boat and go and get the sword and go and kill everyone.'

''Scuse me,' said Scraper.

'Shut up,' said Brat.

'Please.'

'What?'

'Can you take my bukkit off my head? My ears has all swolled up and it's stuck.'

They reached the water's edge and sat on a rock while they decided what to do next.[21] This was the far side of the lake, the furthest bit away from the castle. Camelot itself was more than two miles away, half-

---

[21] *Actually, three of them sat on a rock. Scraper walked into the lake because they hadn't been able to remove his bucket.*

hidden by hundreds of islands dotted everywhere. Some islands were no more than a bit of rock while others, like the Island of Shallot, where Brat had banished the woman he had thought was his mother, but was actually the mother of the real King Arthur, to and had renamed the Island of Vegetables because he kept muddling shallot up with onions, had small buildings on them.

But this part of the lake was deserted. The water was black and dangerous and no one lived here, neither in, nor on, nor by the water. No one even visited there. So there were no boats anywhere, and to make things worse, the clouds had moved since they had seen the rock with Excalibur sticking out of it and the sunlight had gone away. So even if they had got a boat, there was no way they would know which of the more than three hundred islands was the right one. No one even knew exactly how many islands there were, because every time they started counting them, some of them would move. Some islands joined up to make bigger islands while others split into bits making several. This didn't just happen now and then, but all the time, every day, every night, every week, year after year. On still, calm nights, you could actually hear islands banging into each other. This constant smashing and crashing made the islands quite dangerous places to be and because of this, the only people who lived on them were hiding from something or someone that was more frightening than getting squashed by a moving island.

This had all been deliberately done by Merlin's forefathers to protect Excalibur. Only the most determined would ever find it.

'I think we need to plan this,' said Princess Floridian. 'First of all we'll find a new hideout, then we'll steal more money and get a lot of boats and pay some very stupid peasants to row around in them until they find the right place.'

'Wouldn't it be better to pay clever peasants?' said Bloat. 'Wouldn't they find it quicker?'

'They might,' said the Princess. 'But they might also want to keep the enchanted sword for themselves. No, we need people like potato boy here, though probably without buckets on their heads.'

In the meantime Scraper had been blundering around in the lake, tripping over rocks and losing a

couple of toes to hungry olms.[22] The constant falling over in the cold water had made the swelling in his ears go down and finally his bucket came free.

'You are a very bad bukkit,' he said, as he rolled in a bed of thistles to dry himself. 'If bukkit loved me, she would not have made my earholes swell up.'

'OK,' said the Princess, 'rest time's over. Let's go. We need to find a proper hideout.'

They walked round the lake towards Camelot and the main road, which was also a side road and a back road because it was the only road.[23] When they reached it, they hid behind a big rock while they tried to decide what to do next.

'I think the best thing to do would be to make a hideout in the last place anyone would look,' said Bloat.

'What, you mean like on the moon or at the bottom of the lake?' said Brat.

'Or in a really big bukkit?' said Scraper.

'The last place anyone would look is probably a

---

[22] *See* The Dragons 1: Camelot.

[23] *Roads had only been invented ten years before, so there weren't very many of them. In fact there were a lot of people who thought they were a bad idea and would never catch on.*

good idea,' said Princess Floridian. 'As long as it isn't also the first place anyone would look, too. If it wasn't for the seven islands and all the bridges and gatehouses, the best place to have a hideout would be in a nice quiet corner of Camelot itself.'

'There're bits of the castle that no one ever goes to,' said Brat. 'There are all sorts of scary stories about ghosts and demons and vampires living in some of the towers. No one will go near them.'

'They would make the perfect hideout,' said the Princess, 'if we could work out how to get there without having to cross the bridges.'

'But what about the ghosts and demons and vampires?' said Bloat. 'Wouldn't they scare us to death and eat us all up and suck our blood out?'

'Oh come on,' said the Princess. 'These are the Days of Yore, not the Dark Ages. Surely you don't believe all that mumbo jumbo?'

'No, of course not,' said Brat.

'Apart from the ghosts,' said Bloat.

'Well yes, obviously the ghosts,' said Brat. 'We all know they're real.'

'And the demons,' said Scraper.

'Well, yes of course.'

'And the vampires.'

'Naturally,' said Brat, 'we all know they're real.'

Princess Floridian said nothing. She had no time for old-fashioned superstitions, but she herself could remember waking up one morning with all the blood sucked out of her left leg and finding two little puncture marks in her big toe. At the time she had told herself that it had probably just been her nanny, who did have two very pointy teeth and liked to sleep hanging upside down from a wooden beam. She had only been seven and it was ten more years before she found out that all nannies weren't like that.

'So do either of you know a way we can get in and out of the castle undetected?' she said.

'No,' said Brat.

'Yes,' said Bloat.

'Well?'

'The tunnel,' said Bloat.

'Tunnel?'

'The one in the back of the old cave where my granny lives,' said Bloat. 'It goes into the sewers under the castle.'

'Yes, of course,' said Brat.

'So you're saying we can get into the deserted towers,' said the Princess, 'but we have to go up through the lavatory?'

'Yes, brilliant, isn't it?'

'Not so brilliant, actually,' said the Princess.

'Hey,' said Brat, 'it would be the last place anyone would look.'

'That is most definitely true.'

'And besides, no one ever goes there to go there,' said Brat. 'It won't be all gunky and horrible.'

'OK,' said the Princess. 'We'll give it a go. We'll send potato boy up first to clean the pipes with a mop.'

'And my bukkit!' Scraper beamed. 'Yes, let me, let me.'

'Oh, all right,' everyone else agreed.

BEWARE

There is an outbreak of Bagpipes about to sweep the country.
Rabbits and Locusts may eat your gardens,
but Bagpipes will eat your babies.

WHAT TO LOOK OUT FOR:

A very famous dead Irish poet said: 'The best thing about bagpipes
is that they don't smell too.'
HOWEVER, they do have very sharp teeth, can run very fast and
are often covered in Terrible Tartan. The worst thing is the noise. It
is one of the most terrifying and evil sounds on earth.*

WHAT YOU CAN DO:

1. Disguise yourself in even worse Terrible Tartan.
2. Run away very fast.
3. Move to Patagonia.**

At least you can hear them coming and try to hide.
** *There are giant condors in Patagonia that are the only known Bagpipe predators.*

OFFICIAL HEALTH WARNING

Making Plans

Morgan le Fey and Sir Lancelot were in the planning room doing planning. They had a huge map of Avalon spread out on the table and were working out the best way to capture the two mini-rebels and potato boy and rescue the lovely Princess.

Actually, it was Morgan le Fey who was doing all the planning. Sir Lancelot was just nodding and looking all gooey-eyed at her and trying to rehearse the whole troth-plighting thing in his head. All he had was the first verse and he wasn't too pleased with that:

There was a brave knight from Arbroath[24]
Who decided he must plight his troth
But his troth then fell off
And his love said, 'I'm off'.
So he ended up losing them both.

Which he had to admit was pretty terrible and made no sense. He decided he would ask Grimethorpe to write something for him.

---

[24] *Which is a real town in Scotland and one of the few not to have a place in Australia named after it.*

'You know what?' said Morgan le Fey. 'This Princess must be really dumb to have let herself be kidnapped by a couple of children.'

'They must have caught her off guard or threatened her with a dangerous weapon,' said Sir Lancelot.

'Maybe,' said Morgan le Fey, though she had her doubts.

'What? Think you that she may have gone with them of her own free will?'

'Who knows?' said the Princess. 'I think we'll just keep an open mind on that one.'

Neither of them had ever met Princess Floridian, but it was common knowledge that she was a bit of a handful so it did seem unlikely that she would have been overpowered by Brat and his friends.

'Well, everyone knows they were hiding in the old highwayman's cave up the mountain across the valley,' said Morgan le Fey. 'And my spies tell me they were seen leaving there a short while ago. So now we have to try and guess where they're going.'

'I think somewhere near here,' said Sir Lancelot, who actually hadn't the faintest idea where they might

be headed, but put his finger on the map next to Morgan le Fey's.

The gentle touch of fabric as his cuff slid over the back of her hand set her heart fluttering. The map looked all blurry and the Princess felt her knees go all wobbly and uncontrollable. She sat down in a chair and pretended to look out of the window.

'Yes, well,' she said, followed by several large bits of silence.

Gradually her heart regained control of itself and she said, 'We need to work out if they are planning to go to the first place we would look because they think that would be the last place we would look, or if they are planning to go to the last place we would look because they think that would be the last place we would look.'

'Umm, yes, exactly,' said Sir Lancelot, who hadn't the faintest idea what she was talking about.

'Though of course,' the Princess continued, 'they could be going somewhere else completely different where we would never think of looking.'

'Exactly.'

Sir Lancelot was not stupid, by no means, but his

job as a noble knight and executor of fearless deeds did not require a lot of thinking about stuff. In fact, part of his rigorous training had been a month at Avalon's famous Noble Knight And Executor Of Fearless Deeds Boot Camp where all sorts of stuff he wouldn't need had been removed from his brain. These included:

- All long words.
- All his times tables over the number three.
- All the stuff his mother had taught him about personal hygiene.
- Belgian.
- Knitting.
- Lots of other stuff.
- The recipe for rabbit stew.
- More stuff.

Some new things had been implanted in his brain and they included:

- How to make a campfire out of some grass and two damp peasants.
- Killing baddies in dozens of exciting and creative ways.
- How to boil water without burning it.
- The recipe for boiled water.

98

- Belgian.
- Not very much other stuff.
- How to kiss girls, horses and swords, though not necessarily in that order.

So it was not surprising that as Morgan le Fey speculated on the highwaychildren's whereabouts, his eyes glazed over. They had been glazed over before she had started talking due to his being in love with her. So now he was double-glazed.

Morgan le Fey was only single-glazed. She had the being-in-love glazing, but knew exactly what she was talking about even if it wasn't getting her any nearer to finding Brat and Bloat.

'Maybe, my lady,' Sir Lancelot suggested, 'we need some aerial recon ... reconnais ... umm, er.' *Curse those long words*, he thought. 'Something flying about in the sky,' he said.

'What, like a bird?' said Morgan le Fey.

'Well, sort of, except a bird that could follow them and then come back here and tell us where they had gone.'

'Ah, a clever talking bird,' said the Princess. 'Know you of such a bird?'

'Not exactly,' said Sir Lancelot. 'I know of birds and I know of clever things and I know of things that talk, but I do not know of one thing that can do all three.'

'I do,' said Morgan le Fey, 'except it is not a bird.'

'What else does fly, but birds?'

'A vampire.'

'But are not vampires mere fictions?' said Sir Lancelot. 'I know people lived in fear of them in the Dark Ages, but now we are in the Days of Yore and surely people no longer believe in such fairy stories.'

'Except vampires are not fairy stories,' said Morgan le Fey. 'They are rare and secretive and very few have seen them, yet they exist. Not only that, they live right here in Camelot, in the castle itself. Come, I will show you.'

She led Sir Lancelot to the window and pointed across the wide courtyard to a line of towers on the far side. The very highest tower was hidden from view. It was a bright, sunny day, yet a single large cloud encircled the tower like a soft, pale grey cardigan.

'Up there,' she said. 'The tower in the clouds. That is where the vampires live.'

'You have seen them?' asked the knight.

'Indeed I have,' said Morgan le Fey. 'More than seen them, for they have been my friends since I was a baby. On the day I was born, as I lay alone in my crib bathed in the moonlight, they came to me and spoke to me and although I was but a few hours old, I understood their words. They became not only my friends, but my teachers. They taught me all the ancient wisdom of the world, more wisdom than even Merlin himself knows.'

She turned to Lancelot and took his hands in hers.

'You are the only person I have ever told this to,' she said.

Lancelot blushed. He tried to look away, but could not. He tried to speak, but could not. He was desperate to go to the toilet, but could not, which did sore make his eyes water.

'I, umm, I, umm,' he said, but Morgan le Fey put her fingers to his lips.

'You know and I know that we are destined to be together,' she said. 'Your shyness does you credit, my lord. But don't worry, it will pass.'

'Yes, but, yes, but,' Lancelot blurted out. 'I am bursting.'

'I, too, am overwhelmed, but it is our fate,' said Morgan le Fey. 'You must relax and go with the flow.'

Go with the flow was too much. The brave, fearless, noble knight wet himself. He was, however, saved by his cloak and very large boots. He just hoped his beloved would not hear the squelchy noise as he walked about.

Morgan le Fey took a silver whistle from around her neck and blew on it. There was no sound, or rather, the sound it made was way above the range of human hearing, even above the range of dogs, but sure enough, as the two humans looked up into the cloud, a small dot appeared. It circled twice and flew down to their window faster than the human eye could see.

'You have finished your homework, my child?' said the vampire, Fenestra, as she came in through the window.

'No. I'm sorry. I am still working on it,' said Morgan le Fey.

'But it has been three years, my child,' said the vampire.

'I know, I know, but geography's really difficult,' said Morgan le Fey. 'I keep getting stuck in Belgium.'

'Who doesn't?' said Fenestra.

She then noticed Sir Lancelot and froze.

'You know it is forbidden for you to tell anyone of our existence,' she said.

'This is not anyone,' said Morgan le Fey. 'This is Sir Lancelot and we are as one. Our destinies are intertwined forever.'

'Fair enough,' said the vampire. 'I just thought he might be a boyfriend or a servant or something like that, but if your destinies are actually intertwined then that's fine.'

The vampire held out a thin black wing and fluttered her heavy black eyelashes at Sir Lancelot.

'Nice-looking boy, isn't he?' she said. 'Even if he has wet himself.'

Sir Lancelot fainted.[25]

---

[25] *You may have noticed that a lot of people keep fainting in this book. This is because fainting was a new invention in the Days of Yore and looked upon as quite a novelty, which made it very popular and fashionable. It was a huge improvement over the Dark Ages, when throwing up had been all the rage.*

Morgan le Fey explained about Bloat and Brat and how they were trying to find out where they were going.

'I thought maybe you could fly over the area and see if you can spot them,' she said.

'Well, it's not the sort of thing we normally do,' said the vampire. 'I mean, we are a noble race of philosophers, not an HPS[26]. Our minds are focused on higher things than that.'

'What, you mean like sucking blood?' said Morgan le Fey.

'Well, umm, that's just a hobby,' said Fenestra. 'A bit of light relief to break up the endless hours of introspection and doing philosophical stuff.'

'If you find the bandits, you can suck their blood,' said Morgan le Fey, 'as much as you like.'

'Oh, well, that's different then,' said the vampire.

She thought for a bit and then said, 'This bloodsucking, would we be able to do it without having to fill out all the usual forms and endless paperwork?'

In the bad old Dark Ages there were no rules

---

[26] *Highwayman Positioning System.*

controlling bloodsucking, and vampires, who are not known for self-restraint, frequently sucked so much blood out of their victims that they dropped dead.[27] When the Days of Yore started, King Arthur's father, Uther Pendragon, decided something had to be done as everyone was getting fed up tripping over deathly white corpses all the time. So regulations were brought in that meant vampires had to fill out seven forms in triplicate saying exactly when and where and who and lots of other details.[28]

'Yes,' said Morgan le Fey.

'Can you do that? Are you allowed to overrule the rules?'

'I am the King's sister,' said Morgan le Fey. 'I can pretty well do anything I like.'

'All their blood,' said Fenestra, beginning to drool, 'until they are completely white and empty.'

---

[27] *The victims that is, not the vampires. All they got was red teeth and a bit of indigestion.*

[28] *If they finally did get permission to suck blood, there was a very strict formula on how much blood they could take. It was worked out based on the weight of their victim. It was this that had actually led to the invention of diets.*

'Not every last drop. You can make them pale grey, but you must leave them enough to survive. You're not allowed to make them dead,' said Morgan le Fey. 'And you know what that means, don't you?'

'What?'

'When they have made new blood, you can drain them all over again.'

'Wow,' said the vampire. 'And the dragon, we can have his blood too?'

'Oh yes.'

'Gosh, I've never tasted dragon's blood,' said the vampire. 'It's legendary.'

'So you'll do it?' said Morgan le Fey. 'You'll try to find them?'

'Absolutely,' said Fenestra. 'Though could we keep this just between us? I mean, there's only one very small dragon and two humans. If all my twenty-six relatives could suck their blood too, there wouldn't be very much for each of us.'

'So your philosophy doesn't have a problem with selfishness,' Morgan le Fey said with a smile.

'Who cares?' said the vampire. 'Dragon's blood, I mean, come on!'

Morgan le Fey agreed that even if the vampire didn't manage to trace the rebels, but they were found anyway, the vampire could still suck their blood. She realised this meant the vampire could simply sit up in her tower and wait until someone else found them, but Morgan le Fey knew the lure of paperwork-free illicit blood would be strong enough to keep the creature searching all day and all night.

When Sir Lancelot came round, the vampire had left and was already floating back up in her high tower, preparing for her mission.

'We could always go looking ourselves,' said Sir Lancelot. 'On my trusty steed, the magnificent Susan.'

'Yes, but that could take forever,' said Morgan le Fey. 'Even for me it can take half a day just to get across the bridges to the mainland.'

'We do not need to cross the bridges,' said Lancelot.

'Of course we do. How else can we go searching everywhere?'

'Because Susan is no ordinary horse,' said Sir Lancelot. 'She has wings on her heels. She can fly.'

'Yes, right,' said Morgan le Fey. 'You are a

wonderful man who I shall love and respect forever, but flying horses? Come on. This is the Days of Yore, not the Dark Ages when people believed all that sort of hippy stuff.[29] Horses can't fly.'

'But Susan was born in the Dark Ages,' said Sir Lancelot and went over to the window.

This time it was his turn to take a silver whistle from round his neck and blow it. Slowly a large horse that had been grazing in the courtyard below rose into the air. The back of each of her hooves was a blur as eight small wings carried the horse higher and higher. Luckily the window was a big window, so when Susan came level with the sill she simply drifted silently into the room. She walked over to Lancelot and nuzzled him.

Morgan le Fey did not faint. She thought about it and decided fainting was not as fashionable as it had been last week, so decided against it.

'Can she carry both of us?'

---

[29] *Not many people realise that hippies were actually invented centuries ago. Of course a lot of hippies know this as they are still wearing the same clothes and dream of those simple olden days before shampoo and washing machines were invented.*

Susan nodded.

'Can she understand what we're saying?'

Susan nodded again.

'So does she know that we are as one and our destinies are intertwined forever?' said Morgan le Fey.

Susan looked surprised and fainted.[30]

When she came to, she stood up and smiled at Morgan le Fey as only a horse can smile, which is kind of weird. Then she nuzzled the Princess to let her know she was cool with the situation.

I don't think the Princess is ready for a talking horse, Susan thought and winked at Sir Lancelot, who understood perfectly.

---

[30] *One thing she didn't know was that fainting was going out of fashion.*

Home, home on the Drains

eanwhile Brat, Bloat, Princess Floridian and Scraper were approaching the dragons' valley. Until recently it had been a desolate, burnt-out place. Every living plant, from the smallest blades of grass to the great oak trees and everything in between, had been scorched to death by angry dragons breathing fire everywhere, but since Spikeweed, King of the Dragons, had signed the peace treaty with King Arthur, everything had calmed down and the dragons only burnt nasty stinking nettle or prickly things. A good summer of warm rain had worked wonders for the place. The grass was lush and green and tall enough for rabbits to hide in, except for the burnt patches that hadn't been tall enough for rabbits to hide in, where rabbits had thought they were hiding until they were suddenly converted into dinner by a passing dragon.

The trees were heavy with fresh leaves and even a few birds had returned to nest in the topmost branches, where they were out of reach of the dragons' flames. If there is one thing a dragon likes for his tea more than a rabbit, it's a few roasted songbirds. Dragons can fly

and dragons can breathe fire, but they are rubbish at multitasking, so if they try to breathe fire while they are concentrating on flying, they usually burn their own wings which means they crash. The birds knew this and that is why they were safe in the treetops. The birds also knew that it could be really good fun to fly down and sing a lovely song to a dragon until it couldn't contain itself and flew after them up into the treetops and set its own wings on fire.

'I just wish us birds could laugh,' they would tweet to each other as their latest victim fell headfirst onto a big rock.

'We can,' said a kookaburra and laughed so hard it fell off its branch and was crushed to death by a falling dragon.

The four rebels hid behind a rock and looked down into the clearing where most of the dragons lived. Since the peace treaty other dragons had come to the valley. They had come from other countries where humans and dragons were still bitter enemies trying to wipe each other out. The countries included every country that wasn't called Avalon.

'We need to pick a moment when my mum and

dad aren't around,' said Bloat. 'Then we'll creep down and slip into Granny's cave.'

'What about her?' said Princess Floridian. 'Won't she say something?'

'She doesn't even know what planet she's living on,' said Bloat. 'If I tell her we've come to polish her scales, she'll be happy. Actually, if I tell her we are four large bunches of green bananas and have come to her cave to ripen, she'll be happy.'

'What's a banana?' said Scraper. 'Are they dangerous?'

'No, they are cuddly little marsupials,' said Bloat.[31]

'Oh,' said Scraper. 'I spect your granny like them. My granny eated marsupials on toast for her brekfus.'

'That was marmalade, you idiot,' said Princess Floridian.

'Not marmalade,' said Scraper. 'Granny sayed marmalade was evil. No, granny eated baby possums on toast for her brekfus every day.'

'Shut up,' said Brat.

---

[31] *Sarcasm is rare in dragons, but Bloat was particularly good at it.*

113

'Do you want to hear a joke my granny done?' said Scraper.

'No,' said everyone.

'Sometimes she didn't have them on toast, sometimes she boiled them up in a bukkit, not my bukkit of course. She had her own bukkit wot was lovely, but not as lovely as my bukkit which is the loveliest bukkit in the whole world, and you'll never guess what she called it?' said Scraper.

'Marsoupials,' said Princess Floridian.

'Oh, I didn't know you knew my granny.'

'Shut up.'

'I will show your granny my bukkit,' said Scraper. 'Grannies love bukkits.'

'Yes, you do that,' said Bloat. 'Look, there's no one about right now, let's go.'

The four of them crept out from behind the rock and tiptoed down into the cave. No one saw them except for two people flying through the clouds on a horse. Fortunately the two people were Morgan le Fey and Sir Lancelot and the horse was the wonderful Susan. Fenestra did not see them. She was back in her tower getting ready to begin the search. Vampires are

notoriously vain and will not go anywhere without sharpening their claws and covering their skin in a protective layer of magical grease to attract evil spirits.[32]

The ancient dragon was sleeping in a very large puddle at the back of the cave. King Arthur had given the dragons a large supply of incontinence pants for the old granny when they had signed their peace treaty, but even wearing three pairs of Super Strong Leakylegs was not enough to contain the endless stream of wee that leaked out of the ancient creature. The smell was so powerful that it made the visitors' eyes sting and burnt the back of their throats.

Although she was fast asleep and snoring like a hippopotamus with a very bad sinus problem, the minute the three runaways got within three metres of her she shook herself and spoke.

'I smells visitors,' she said. 'A boy, a lovely grandson, a lovely Princess and a big lovely walking

[32] *This grease comes from a very remote mountain in Patagonia where it oozes from a crevice on a cliff top. Western chemists managed to synthesise this grease in 1922. They called it Vegemite and then lied to everyone about how it was made from yeast. The truth is so gross even I can't bring myself to tell you what it's really made of.*

potato with a lovely bucket.'

'Hello, Granny,' said Bloat. 'We came to see how you were.'

'Who's that?' said the old dragon. 'Is it young Bloat?'

'No, he's not here at all,' said Bloat. 'It's me, Clarence, Bloat's cousin.'

'Clarence?'

'Yes, Granny,' said Bloat as the four of them tiptoed past the old creature towards the tunnel entrance.

'Why are you all tiptoeing past me towards the tunnel entrance? Anyone would think you hadn't come to visit me at all and just wanted to go into the drains.'

'Oh Granny, how could you think such a thing?' said Bloat.

'Because it's true,' said the old dragon. 'No one comes to see me any more except Wee Blind Jock.'

'And we all know he's not real, don't we, Granny?'

'Of course he is. Look at all the wee on the floor. That's Wee Blind Jock, that is. He comes every night and cocks his leg on me. How else do you think all this wee gets here?'

The old dragon opened her eyes and tried to breathe fire, but all that came out of her nose was a puff of damp black smoke.

'I must get my nostrils cleaned out,' she said. 'They're all full of clinker. I don't suppose you could do it, could you? I've got a wire brush and if you do, I'll let you touch my magic wart.'

'Hey, look,' said Brat, pointing towards the cave entrance. 'Here comes Wee Blind Jock now.'

As the old dragon turned to look they ran away down the tunnel.

'Hello, Wee Blind Jock,' they could hear Bloat's granny say. 'Come over here and speak up. I can't hear you because you're blind.'

'Are you sure this is the only way in and out of this tower?' said Princess Floridian. 'I don't think I can go through all that rubbish every time.'

'Once we get set up in the tower, we can get Bloat to fly us in and out,' said Brat. 'We'll just have to wait until it's dark.'

'Can you see in the dark?' the Princess asked Bloat.

'Of course I can,' said the young dragon. 'It's easy.

117

I mean, it's only one colour, just a big black thing.'

Princess Floridian began to wonder if the whole pretending-to-be-kidnapped thing had been such a good idea. Maybe it would have been better to have beaten up the useless highwaymen and gone on to King Arthur's coronation. Who knows, she might have ended up becoming Mrs King Arthur. She knew that boys found her irresistible and OK, so the King was only eleven years old, but she could wait. In five years' time he would be eighteen,[33] the same as her. Of course this could still happen. She could beat up Brat and Bloat, stuff Scraper's bucket over his head again and drag them all back to Camelot.

She would be a hero and *everyone* would want to marry her. She'd probably get a big reward too. But there was a bigger reward waiting to be claimed and she was determined to get it.

EXCALIBUR.

Excalibur was the stuff legends were made of and then

---

[33] *Princess Floridian: staggeringly beautiful, super-intelligent, fluent in five languages, great cook, but completely terrible at maths.*

some. Children everywhere, not just in Avalon, but all over the world, knew about the magical sword. Thousands of them dreamt of the day plastic would be invented so they could have a model of their own. Sure, there were cardboard[34] Excaliburs, but owning one of them always ended in tears. You would be out playing knights and damsels with all the other children and it would start raining, and before you knew it your Excalibur was a limp soggy mess with everyone laughing at it.

No, the Princess had seen the beam of sunlight shine down through the clouds on the mighty sword and she was determined that one way or another she would be the one to claim it. Legend said that whoever pulled it out of the rock would be the one true owner of the sword and its incredible powers and no one would ever be able to take it off you. Of course she could go and tell King Arthur about seeing the sword, but if she

---

[34] *In case you think cardboard didn't exist in the Days of Yore, it was actually invented by the ancient Chinese, who treated it as a food item – a tradition still carried on by many fast food shops to this day. For example, next time you buy a takeaway burger try throwing the burger away and eating the cardboard box. You will be pleasantly surprised.*

did that, there would be no way she would be allowed to own it. No, her best chance was to use the idiots she was with to lead her to it. Brat might think he would be the chosen one, but Princess Floridian decided that once they found the right island, she would have no problem claiming ownership.

She would just kill the other three.

They reached the place where the tunnels led into the drains beneath Camelot. There were hundreds of pipes leading down from the castle. All the toilets, baths, basins, rainwater pipes and other leaky things like the blood pipes from the ancient torture chambers and the cheese overflows from the mighty pizza ovens fed into this one huge drain that flowed away into a darkness no one had ever explored. It was rumoured to run into the very core of the world itself, though a race of natives living on an undiscovered island somewhere in the South Seas knew otherwise. From the top of their single mountain, the most disgusting stream imaginable poured down over a great brown waterfall into their valley. The air was permanently filled with the aroma of ancient sewage and boiled cabbage and old blood and pizza. Of course, the natives had never known anything else, so to them it was the river of life and it made their land so rich they grew potatoes the size of footballs.[35] They tasted absolutely awful, but they were enormous.

Luckily, Bloat had been one of the young dragons who had blown bubbles up into the toilets of Camelot[36] so he knew which drain led up into the remote tower where they were to make their hideout.

'Me go, me go first, please, please,' said Scraper jumping up and down with excitement. 'Bukkit all ready to clean up.'

'All right,' said Brat, 'as you have been such a good boy, we will let you go up first.'

'Thank you, thank you, thank you,' said Scraper. 'Me and bukkit will make so clean and shiny you could eat your dinner off it.'

'Great,' said Brat.

'Shouldn't you have some sort of brush?' said the Princess.

---

[35] *The only trouble was that they tasted like footballs too, but that was nowhere near as bad as the taste of the fish from the river. We will not go there, but if you ever eat one of these fish, you will be going everywhere, very, very, frequently.*

[36] *See* The Dragons 1: Camelot.

'Got hairy arms,' said Scraper. 'Better than brush.'

He forced himself into the pipe and began to wriggle upwards.

'Well, if he can get up there, we'll have no problem,' said Brat.

Half an hour is not a very long time when you are enjoying yourself. However, if you are standing in an enormous sewer as all sorts of unmentionable things float past you, some of which reach out and try to grab your ankle, half an hour is a very long time indeed.

While Scraper worked his way up the pipe, two half an hours went by. Now and then something fell out of the pipe – one of Scraper's boots, two small crocodiles and a lot of brown things followed by nothing. The nothing went on for another ten minutes.

'I hope he's not stuck,' said the Princess.

'Well, if he is, there's nothing we can do about it,' said Brat.

'I realise that,' said the Princess. 'I don't care if he does get stuck, except *if* he does we won't be able to get up into the tower.'

But as she began to say more, an enormous flash of water shot out of the pipe followed by Scraper.

'Brilliant way to get down,' he said with a grin. 'Just flushed meself.'

'So it's all nice and clean?' said the Princess. 'We can go up?'

'Oh yes,' said Scraper. 'Queen could eat her dinner off toilet pipe.'

One by one they all wriggled up the pipe with Scraper at the back in case any of the others lost their grip and slipped down. With potato boy there they would have something soft to land on and not fall all the way down to the bottom.

One by one they climbed out of the toilet bowl, except Scraper, who could only get his arm up into the room.

'Well, we can either flush him down again or smash the lavatory and get him out,' said Bloat.

'I think we should smash it,' said Princess Floridian, 'but before we do, can you boys leave the room while I use it?'

'What about Scraper?' said Bloat. 'I think we should warn him.'

'Scraper, can you hear me?' the Princess shouted.

'Yes.'

123

'Have you got your bucket?'

'Of course I have.'

'Well, put it on your head.'

'Why?'

'You'll see.'

'Bukkit might get stuck again,' said Scraper.

The Princess explained why and Scraper agreed that getting his head stuck in his bucket was probably the nicer option.

Good Citizens of Avalon,
do you suffer from
Bukkit Deficiency?
Well, buy yourself a
**Sir Lancepot
De-Luxe Bukkit today***

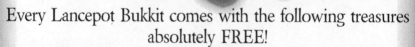

Every Lancepot Bukkit comes with the following treasures
absolutely FREE!
1. Seepage.
2. Germs (lethal and non-lethal).
3. Your choice of two smells from our new, exciting
Fresh Sewage range.

***PLEASE NOTE**: Bubonic Plague Infection carries a 9 Groat surcharge.

*As thrown up in by Royalty in seventeen different countries.

Up, up and away on my beautiful . . . Horse?

'**W**hy would they go to the Dragon Valley?' said Sir Lancelot as they circled around on Susan's back. 'The little dragon's parents will be looking out for him.'

'Exactly,' said Morgan le Fey. 'So that means they are going to hide in the last place they think we would look for them.'

'They've gone into that cave,' said Sir Lancelot. 'So all we have to do is fly down there and grab them.'

'I think not. I think that is the cave with the tunnel at the back that leads into the castle drains. I don't think they're going to hide in the Dragon Valley. I think they are planning to hide in Camelot itself.'

'That is brilliant,' said Lancelot. 'I know they are highwaymen and all that and we want to capture them, but what a brilliant bit of strategy, hiding not so much under our noses as right up our noses.'

'Quite,' said Morgan le Fey. 'Too bloody clever by half. There are over a hundred drains going down into the sewers. It could take weeks to find them.'

'We'll place guards in the cave,' she added, 'but I

think once they get into the castle they'll find another way to get in and out.'

Morgan le Fey had been an independent free-thinker all her life. Someone only had to tell her not to do something for her to want to do it. Her parents and teachers had thought this would be the easiest way to get her to do something *they* wanted her to do, but which *she* didn't want to do. However, the Princess was far too clever for that and usually beat them at their own game. If there was something she wanted to do, maybe stay out late to watch a Wild Minstrel sing rude songs, then she would first of all pretend it was the last thing in the world she would ever want and then make her guardians believe that being made to do it would actually be really, really good for her education.

This was what is known as a win, win, win situation because:

1. Morgan le Fey would get to hear the Wild Minstrel.

2. Her parents would believe they had made her go when she really hadn't wanted to, which meant they thought they were actually in charge when they weren't.

3.   Her parents would even believe the Wild
      Minstrel's rude songs had taught her a lot of
      wonderful, useful new knowledge when in fact
      all they had taught her were a lot of wonderful,
      useful new swear words.

Part of her rebellion had been to go to places she was specifically told not to go to. This included all of the Remote Wing of Camelot, a collection of corridors and towers that had been almost deserted since the Terrible Hauntings And Turning Into Frogs that had taken place two hundred and fifty years before.

The Terrible Hauntings And Turning Into Frogs had never happened. The whole thing had been created by Merlin's grandmother to get some peace and quiet. She had got so fed up with people bothering her all day with requests for spells and potions to cure everything from The Purple Plague to Belgian Ague With Added Sauce that she had begun to tell stories of terrifying ghosts that had started appearing in the Remote Wing.

This had confused the people living in the Remote Wing, which in those days had been known

as the remote wing and had been a peaceful, laid-back sort of place. They had never seen a single ghost. So Merlin's grandmother began wandering around at night covered in a white sheet, wailing painfully and chucking lots of frogs about. This had been back in the Dark Ages and in those days people had been very gullible and superstitious.[37] In no time at all the remote wing was deserted because everyone living there had fled.

Once they had all gone, Merlin's grandmother, Grannivere, moved in and no one bothered her ever again. She gradually faded from everyone's memory and if her name cropped up now, it was assumed that she had died a long, long time ago. After all, Merlin himself was very, very old and his mother Mummivere had died many years before. So his granny must have died long, long ago.

She hadn't.

And the one and only person who knew she was still alive was Morgan le Fey, because she was the one and only person who had been brave enough to venture

---

into the Remote Wing since it had been abandoned.[38] She had been all over the Remote Wing because she had been told it was the most dangerous place in the whole world and she must never, never go anywhere near it.

'And if I was them that's where I would go and hide,' she said.

'If that's the case,' said Sir Lancelot, 'they are unassailable.'

'No they're not,' said Morgan le Fey.

'Well, it won't matter anyway. Everyone knows the Remote Wing is the most dangerous place in the whole world and no one must ever, ever go anywhere near it,' said the brave and fearless knight.

'That's just a myth.'

'No, no, it's not,' said Lancelot. 'Everyone knows it is a terrifying place that no one ever comes back from because they have been haunted to death by big white ghosts and ferocious frogs.'

'How long have you lived at Camelot?'

'Five years,' said Sir Lancelot, 'though I was away

---

[38] *Actually, one other person had been there: Brat, the fake King Arthur. He had gone there to use the toilet, but he had only gone into the very first bit of it and had kept his eyes shut.*

doing noble deeds for four years, eleven months and three weeks.'

'I was born here,' said Morgan le Fey. 'There is not a single room that I have not been to. Apart from the Secret and Hidden Rooms that I have not visited because they are secret and hidden and may not actually exist, but I have been all over Camelot including the Remote Wing, into every room and corridor and cupboard lots and lots of times. Well, I've only been into the cupboards once, but I've been into the corridors and rooms tons of times.'

'And the frogs didn't get you?'

'Does it look like they did?'

'It must be because you are a royal Princess. I expect the great and wise Merlin gave you a special protection spell when you were born,' said Sir Lancelot.

'Or,' said Morgan le Fey, 'and this is just a suggestion based on the fact I've been there lots and lots of times, there are no frogs.'

'But . . .'

'Or ghosts.'

'But . . .'

'Not a single one. And there is someone living

there,' said the Princess. 'Someone who will not be at all pleased to find she has visitors.'

'Who?'

'Grannivere, Merlin's grandmother.'

Sir Lancelot thought about it. He began to wonder if Morgan le Fey had maybe drunk too much strange mushroom tea that morning and it was affecting her brain. He hoped that was the case.

Otherwise, he thought, *I have fallen in love with a looney.*

'But she would have to be over two hundred years old,' said Lancelot.

'Two hundred and eighty-seven, to be precise,' said Morgan le Fey. 'Her birthday was last Thursday. I made her a cake.'

Now Sir Lancelot knew he was in love with a crazy person.

'OK,' he said. 'Susan, I think we should go back to the castle now.'

Even Susan thought Morgan le Fey was probably mad. She had flown past the Remote Wing, at a safe distance, quite a few times and had never seen any sign of life apart from thick cobwebs over the windows.

'But then again, if there are giant frogs there,' Susan said out loud before she could stop herself, 'there wouldn't be any cobwebs because the frogs would have eaten all the spiders.'

'Did that horse just speak?' said Morgan le Fey.

'Sorry,' said Susan. 'Didn't mean to startle you.'

OMW,[39] thought the Princess, *I have fallen in love with a strange man who has a mad talking horse.*

Luckily, Susan was wearing her self-righting saddle, the one with the velvet seatbelts, otherwise Morgan le Fey would have fallen off with surprise. Nevertheless Susan flew back to Camelot as quickly as possible.

There were seventy-four towers in the Remote Wing and some of them were more than twenty-three stories high. To search all of them would take ages.

'And of course if they got any idea we were looking for them, they could just keep moving around so we'd never find them,' Morgan le Fey. 'What we need is a spy.'

'I could fly around and look through the windows,' said Susan.

---

[39] *Oh My Wizard.*

'Yes. I think a big flying horse looking in the window at them might make them a bit suspicious.'

'Well, I could pretend I hadn't seen them.'

'Umm, that's one option,' said Morgan le Fey. 'But I think we need someone a bit smaller.'

'Or someone disguised as something else,' Sir Lancelot suggested.

'Yes, you could tie feathers all over me and I could pretend I was a bird,' said Susan.

'I think you'll find most birds weigh quite a bit less than a thousand kilos,' said Morgan le Fey. 'Probably about nine hundred and ninety-nine kilos less.'

'I wasn't thinking of feathers,' said Sir Lancelot. 'I was thinking of a bit of trompe l'oeil.'

'I'm not being covered in dead fish,' said Susan.

'It means trick of the eye,' said Lancelot. 'I was thinking of painting you to look like a big cloud.'

Morgan le Fey went to the window and blew her vampire whistle. When Fenestra arrived she explained the situation. How they'd seen the runaways going into the dragon's cave and where she thought they were probably headed. She told the vampire that with a bit

of luck she could be in for a nice bit of bloodsucking quite soon, once they could find out exactly which tower they had taken refuge in.

'I have the perfect solution,' said the vampire. 'My nephew Fissure. He's only eight years old and he's so small for his age you could easily mistake him for a crow. Give him a couple of plump rats to suck dry and he'll fly round every tower in Camelot, not just the ones in the Remote Wing.

'Because, I know you think that's where they might be,' Fenestra continued, 'but I'm not so sure. For a start they might think that you might think that's where they would probably go, so they won't. And secondly, they probably know all the myths about the Remote Wing and might be too scared to go there.'

'You could be right, but Brat has been there before,' said Morgan le Fey. 'To go to the lavatory when the young dragons were blowing bubbles at him.'[40]

While the Princess sent down to the kitchens for a pair of plump fresh rats, Fenestra flew back to her tower to fetch Fissure. The young vampire had never

---

[40] *See* The Dragons 1: Camelot.

seen two plump fresh rats at the same time before and his eyes lit up like small fires. He began to drool and tremble in anticipation and would have eaten his own mother if he'd been asked to.[41]

'You can drain one rat now,' said the old vampire, 'and have the other one when you find them.'

'And if you find them nice and quickly, you might even get a third rat too,' Morgan le Fey added.

'Wow, I'll be as quick as lightning,' said Fissure, though it sounded more like: 'Mmmmmm urggh ooh yummmmm,' because he had both fangs in a rat's neck.

The young vampire flew off towards the Remote Wing. From where she stood at the window, Morgan le Fey could just make him out as a tiny black dot flying round and round the towers like an eccentric corkscrew as he spiralled down from the top windows to the bottom. He shot round a dozen towers in less

---

[41] *It was actually an old vampire tradition to murder relatives and drink their blood. It was a tradition that had begun in the Very Dark Ages which had come before the Dark Ages, when all sorts of unspeakable things were frequently spoken about. On the positive side, it was a very effective way of keeping vampire numbers quite low, and you wouldn't want thousands of them everywhere sticking their fangs into all your soft bits, would you?*

than five minute and then vanished. He flew round the back of the farthest tower to begin the corkscrew, but didn't reappear.

'I wish someone would invent a long cardboard tube with a bumpy glass bit at each end that would make things that are a long way away look as if they were much nearer,' said Morgan le Fey.

'No one would buy anything like that,' said Sir Lancelot.

'I just wish someone would invent cardboard,' said the vampire. 'At least that would be a start.'[42]

'I think my mother did invent cardboard,' said Sir Lancelot, who had not read footnote 34, 'but she called it an omelette.'

'They could call it a muchcloserscope,' said Morgan le Fey.

'I think omelette sounds better,' said Lancelot.

'I hope he's all right,' said the vampire when her nephew still had not reappeared ten minutes later.

I hope he's not, thought the second rat.

---

[42] *See footnote 34.*

AN AMAZING
INCREDIBLE
EVENT
is coming soon,
VERY, VERY SOON.

THE EXCITING,
THE AMAZING,
THE INCREDIBLE

PAGE 140
is
ALMOST
HERE!

Turn over and it will be revealed . . .

Crackpot

After they had smashed the toilet, helped Scraper out of the drain and pulled the bucket off his head, they reviewed their situation.

'Right,' said Princess Floridian. 'This is the situation.'

'No, I think it's the bathroom,' said Scraper.

Brat and Bloat agreed with him.

I wish I'd listened to my teacher more, the Princess thought, *when she said never work with children, animals and walking potatoes.*

'Before we go any further,' the Princess continued, 'I think there will be a new rule and anyone who breaks it will get a punch in the ear.'

'A punch?' said Scraper. 'Isn't that a fing for making holes in bukkits?'

'No,' said Princess Floridian, holding up a rusty gadget for making holes in leather belts. 'It's one of these and every time you break the rule you will get yet another place in your ear where you can put a big fat earring.'

'But …' Scraper began, followed by a loud scream of pain.

'You haven't said what the rule is,' said Brat, backing away behind Bloat.

'So I haven't,' said the Princess. 'Sorry, potato boy, you have a one-hole credit. The rule is that none of you can speak a single word unless I say you can.'

'But . . .' Scraper began and then stopped very suddenly.

'That's your credit used up,' said the Princess. 'So if I ask any of you a question, then of course, you can speak, and if something is creeping up behind me and looks dangerous you may speak. Every other time, you must put your hand in the air and wait.'

Bloat put his wing in the air.

'Yes?'

'I haven't got any hands,' said the young dragon.

He put his wing in the air again.

'Yes?'

'It probably isn't dangerous, but there's a small black bird sitting on the windowsill looking at us,' said Bloat.

Princess Floridian spun round and tried to grab the bird, but the little vampire, who looked like a bird, was too quick for her.

142

'Have you been sent here to spy on us?' she said.

'No,' said Fissure. 'Why, what are you doing?'

'None of your . . . ow, ow, ow,' cried Brat as the Princess punched a hole in his ear.

'Well, what are you doing here?' she said.

'Just flying about,' said Fissure. 'Us birds do that a lot, flying about. It's probably what we do best of all.'

'Bird?' said the Princess. 'I thought you were a vampire bat.'

'Funny you should say that,' said the young bat. 'I get that all the time.'

'Would you like to spy for us?' said the Princess.

'Might do,' said Fissure, thinking if he played his cards right, he could become a double-agent and get double rats. 'What's in it for me?'

'What would you like?' said Princess Floridian.

'Ah, well,' said Fissure.

Because he was supposed to be a bird he was supposed to like all the gross stuff that birds ate like seeds and flowers and other planty things. He knew that birds did not suck the blood out of things.

If I ask for a rat, he thought, *they might get suspicious.*

143

He knew some birds did eat rats, but they were usually quite dead rats that had bits fallen off from rotting and no blood left inside at all.

'What have you got?' he said.

'OK, guys, you may speak,' said the Princess. 'Any suggestions?'

'You could sit on my bukkit for a bit,' said Scraper.

'Some cheese?' said Brat.

'Have you got any cheese?'

'No,' said Brat, 'but I have got a sausage.'

'Sausage?' said Fissure, who wasn't sure what a sausage was on account of them not being part of the standard vampire diet, which was mainly made up of blood with the addition of more blood. 'What's that then?'

'It's a brilliant new invention,' said Brat. 'I stole it from the castle kitchen before I escaped. You take a tube out of a dead animal's stomach then you cut up bits of another dead animal or even several dead animals and mash them up with things like fat and blood and onions and bread and plants and then you stuff them inside the tube you got out of the dead stomach and then boil them.'

'That is gross,' said Princess Floridian. 'No one would eat that.'

'They do,' said Brat. 'They're really fashionable and they have a special thing to cook them on called a BarbYeCue.'

'Did you say it had blood in it?' said Fissure.

'Yes, loads of it,' said Brat. 'It's a blood sausage.'

'All right,' said Fissure. 'I'll do it.'

'Good boy,' said the Princess.

'What is it I'm going to do?' said the young bat, who couldn't think of anything except the blood sausage.

'Be our spy,' said the Princess.

'Right,' said Fissure. 'What am I going to spy on then?'

'Everything.'

'Right. So when do I get the sausage?'

'Every time you tell us something useful, I will give you a slice.'

'Right, I'll get started right away,' said Fissure.

'Oh, and one thing before you go,' said Princess Floridian as casually as she could. 'It's not important, but um, er, I don't suppose you've seen a sort of sword

145

thing sticking out of a bit of a rock out in the lake somewhere, have you?'

'Do you want me to spy on it?'

'Well, only if you happen to see it,' said the Princess. 'It's not for me, you understand, but I've got a friend who absolutely loves swords and he'd be quite sort of excited, well, no, excited is too strong a word. I mean he . . .'

'Your friend?'

'Yes, my friend. He'd be quite interested to know where it is,' said the Princess.

'Oh.'

'So if you happen to see this sort of sword thing, you know, when you're flying around over the lake around all those lovely little islands, my friend would be rather sort of happy to know where it is. I think it belonged to a friend of his who might have dropped it or something like that.'

'So it belongs to your friend's friend then?' said Fissure.

'That's it,' said the Princess. 'And he's a good friend of mine. I don't mean my friend's friend – I've never met him – I mean my friend. So it would be

146

really nice if we could find the sword for him.'

'OK.'

'I would think he – my friend, that is – would be so pleased if you did find it that he would want me to give you an extra slice of blood sausage, if you found his friend's sword, that is.'

'OK,' said Fissure. 'Say no more. I'm on the case.'

And with that he flew off over the lake and all the islands.

Bats
an infomercial

A lot of people think that vampire bats were once human beings that were turned into vampires one night while they were asleep and a vampire flew into their room and bit them in the neck. This is both true and completely wrong because there are vampires and vampire bats.[43]

Here are the dictionary definitions:

vampire *n.*   **1.** a corpse supposed, in European folklore, to leave its grave at night to drink the blood of the living by biting their necks with long pointed canine teeth. This then turns their victims into vampires or, worse still, geography teachers or, even worser, geography teachers in corduroy jackets who teach their students about Belgium and nowhere else. **2.** See **vampire bat.**

---

[43] *There are also Batty Vampires, which are vampires that have gone mad, and Batty Vampire Bats, which are vampire bats that have gone mad. There are also Umpire Bats, which are bats that like cricket.*

> **vampire bat** *n.* a small bat that feeds on the blood of mammals, birds and humans,[44] using its two sharp incisor teeth and anticoagulant saliva, found mainly in tropical America, Manhattan and Avalon. Contrary to a widely held misunderstanding among book editors and other people, vampire bats do not change into people. They are bats all the time.

Avalon had both types of vampire, but the ones we are concerned with now are the vampire bats. There are no vampire graves inside Camelot itself. They are all in a small town by the seaside called Byton Bay where people go on holiday to lose weight by having a couple of pints of blood sucked out of them and get a nice tan.

Vampire bats, on the other hand, do not live in graves because they are not human corpses. They are small furry mammals that hang upside down from beams in the towers of big castles like Camelot. They are actually quite soft and cuddly. It's just that they

---

[44] *Not to be confused with the Vampire Fish, which sucks the insides out of tadpoles.*

150

drink blood – and who hasn't done that now and then? Actually, even if they don't suck your blood, their bite alone can give you some very unpleasant diseases. There is one called Lyssavirus which kills you and another called Rabies[45] which makes you froth at the mouth and kills you, but you don't really mind because you've already gone completely insane.

The Vampires of Camelot[46] have lived in the castle since it was first built and are the oldest vampire family on earth. Many people believe that all the world's vampires are descended from the Vampires of Camelot. Where they came from, no one knows. Many people believe they were created by Merlin's great-great-grandfather Merlin.

'It's the sort of thing he might have done,' they say. 'After all, anyone who created something as evil as cats would be capable of anything.'

'I didn't know Merlin created cats,' other people say.

---

[45] *Not to be confused with Babies which, although very dangerous, don't bite you so much and usually do the mouth frothing thing themselves.*

[46] *Now there's a brilliant title for a rubbish TV series.*

'Oh yes, he made the first one out of some rusty barbed-wire, a piece of broken glass, a cup of spit and something an owl coughed up.'

'Wow. You learn something new every day.'

'No you don't.'

The oldest vampire in Camelot was three hundred and fifty-seven. She was called Lucestays and she never left her beam in the bat tower of Camelot. Her legs and wings were so stiff with arthritis she could barely move them, and it had been over fifty years since she had swooped down on a sleeping creature to suck its blood. Nowadays her children would go out, grab a mouse, carry it back to the tower and hold it for her while she had a bit of a drink. Her fangs were so worn down that her children even had to make the puncture holes for her.

'I should have died years ago,' she kept saying.

No one argued with her, even though they were the ones keeping her alive without realising they were actually doing it. It was the mice they brought her every few days. The *Muris immortalis cametloticus* or Camelot Everlasting Mouse, a creature that had definitely been created by one of the early Merlins,

actually contained the secret of immortality in its blood. A few drops could stop you ageing for up to a month[47] and as Lucestays drank the blood once a week, she simply stopped getting any older. The only person who knew this was Merlin himself as he also sucked on an Everlasting Mouse once a week. There were also a few very, very old cats around the castle.

Lucestays was actually getting a tiny bit older because sometimes her children brought back a baby rat by mistake and that blood did not have any magical qualities apart from giving you really bad wind.

By and large the vampires kept themselves to themselves. They usually only left their tower at night and most people didn't believe they actually existed. It suited the vampires that way because by and large people tend to look upon bloodsucking in a disapproving sort of way. If they had known there was a big family of vampires in the neighbourhood, they would have all gone to bed with their socks on because, as everyone knows, ankles are a vampire's favourite feeding place.

---

[47] *In hot weather this was reduced to about eight days.*

'Humans are ridiculous,' said Fenestra. 'I mean, how many of them have actually tasted fresh warm blood? As we all know, if they did they would realise just how incredibly delicious it is.'

Morgan le Fey was the great exception to the rule. On the day she had been born, Fenestra had come to her as she lay in her crib beside the bed of her sleeping mother. What exactly had brought the bat to the child's side is a mystery. As the child had come into the world, Fenestra, who had been hanging from her Friday Beam[48] dreaming of a red Christmas, which is like a white Christmas only with a lot more blood, had felt something calling her. It was not a voice, but something in her soul, a feeling more than a noise, and the calling came from Morgan le Fey. For her part the newborn princess was unaware of it, yet when Fenestra flew down and sat on her chest looking deep into her eyes, the child knew there was a bond that would tie the two of them together forever. From that day on there was barely a day when the two of them didn't

---

[48] *Most of the older bats had a different beam to hang from for every day of the week. The reason is far too complicated to go into here, but has something to do with woodworm and dry-rot.*

speak to each other. Fenestra became the secret eyes and ears, bringing secrets from all around Camelot to the young princess, secrets that she stored away in her memory, secrets that were there to use whenever she needed them.

Fenestra's friends and relations were Morgan le Fey's friends too and watched over her wellbeing day and night. Now that Sir Lancelot had come into her life, they watched over her day and night and knight.

There were two hundred and fifty-eight vampires living at Camelot and every night they spread out across the countryside looking for warm ankles. Only Lucestays and the baby vampires stayed behind. The baby vampires were still being fed by their mothers so they didn't need fresh blood. However, to make sure they knew what to do when they were old enough to go out and feed, each baby was left with a big red tomato to practise biting on.

Sausages – Fact or Fiction?

Fissure flew out over the lake until he was out of sight of the runaways. He looked down over the islands, without really paying much attention.

Excalibur, he thought, *boring*.

Then he swung round, making sure he couldn't be seen, and flew back to Morgan le Fey and Lancelot.

'They're looking for Excalibur,' he said.

'Who isn't?' said Sir Lancelot.

'Indeed, my lord,' said Morgan le Fey. 'People have searched for the Sword of the True King for hundreds of years.'

'Are you sure?' said the vampire.

'Absolutely,' said Morgan le Fey. 'Why do you ask?'

'Well, all you had to do was ask us vampires. We all know where it is. Always have. For all the good it will do you,' said the vampire.

'Why do you say that?' said Sir Lancelot.

'Well, I know of at least eighty-three people who have tried to pull it out of the rock and I've no doubt there are dozens more, but no one has moved it as much as a hair's width.'

'That is because it is the Sword of the True King,' said Morgan le Fey. 'Only he can pull it from the stone.'

'Your father couldn't,' said the vampire, 'and he was a true King. I mean, they didn't come much truer than Uther Pendragon, good friend to us vampires he was. That's why we showed him where the sword was, but even he failed to move it.'

'My father tried to remove Excalibur?'

'He did indeed. He burst several blood vessels trying and put his back out so badly he had to lie down on a plank of wood for a whole month with unguents down his trousers, and even after that, he forever walked with a slight limp and a strange tilt to the south.'

'So that's how he got that,' said the Princess. 'He always told me it was an old war wound from a battle with a giant phoenix.'

'There's no such thing as a giant phoenix,' said the vampire.

'I know that,' said Morgan le Fey, 'but I thought that was because my father had killed it.'

'They asked me to spy for them,' said Fissure.

'What, the boy Brat?' said Morgan le Fey.

'No, the one who's in charge,' said Fissure. 'The girl.'

'Girl? There isn't a girl . . .' the Princess began. 'No! The girl? It has to be that poor King Kasterwheel's daughter that he thought they had kidnapped. Well, well.'

'Should we send for him?' said Sir Lancelot.

'Tricky,' said the Princess. 'He thinks his daughter is an angel. I think the shock would give him a heart attack. On the other hand it would be better he find out from us rather than tittle-tattle gossip from the servants.'

When King Kasterwheel arrived, Morgan le Fey sat him down in a comfy chair, gave him a nice big cup of super-relaxing chamomile tea and broke the news to him that his sweet, innocent daughter was actually a nasty, greedy, selfish little minx.

'Oh yes,' said the King. 'I could have told you that.'

'Oh,' said Morgan le Fey. 'I thought you would be devastated.'

'Devastated? Oh no, my dear. I passed devastated years ago. I'm on depressed resignation now,' he said.

159

'From the day she was born she has been possessed by wickedness. She hid it behind her great beauty and immense charm and fooled almost everyone.'

'So what has she done?' said Morgan le Fey.

'Our daughter was five years old and for her birthday party we employed a travelling circus, and that day my wife ran away with a clown,' said the King, 'All she left me was a short note burnt into the fur of our daughter's teddy bear. It said, "Boodgye". I knew my wife had no great talent at spelling and so I believed she had deserted me forever. It was not until our daughter's nursemaid came to me and explained that Boodguy was one of the circus clowns that I understood. I was devastated. My wife had deserted us for a short dumpy bald clown with enormous shoes and a huge red nose.'

'You poor man,' said Morgan le Fey. 'That is terrible.'

'Would that that was the whole story,' said the King.

'There's more?'

'Indeed. A few years later I discovered that my wife had not run away at all,' the King explained. 'Our daughter, the angelic Floridian, had killed her.'

160

'A five-year-old child?' said Morgan le Fey.

'Indeed. Somehow she got her mother to stand behind one of the circus elephants and then fed it a currant bun, knowing full well that elephants always sit down to eat buns. My wife was squashed flat. Floridian then bribed Boodguy the Clown with an enormous bag of jelly babies to push the body into the moat.'

'How did you find this out?'

'The clown confessed on his death bed,' said the King. 'I have not told my daughter that I know her secret, but nothing she does will surprise me, except perhaps being nice.'

'You poor man,' said Morgan le Fey.

'Well, actually I am seriously rich,' said King Kasterwheel. 'I'm just a bit crap in my personal relationships.'

'We need to make a plan,' said Sir Lancelot. 'You are sure the girl is the one in charge?'

'Absolutely,' said Fissure. 'The others do whatever she tells them, even the big one that looks like a potato.'

'And she wants to find Excalibur?'

'Yes, but she pretended she didn't really want to, she was just looking for it as a favour to a friend who

also wasn't that interested,' said Fissure. 'I just **acted** dumb, so now I am spying for them.'

'What are they going to pay you with?' Morgan le Fey asked. 'More rats?'

'A sausage.'

'A sausage?' said the Princess. 'Do you know that they've got a ruby worth ten million gold crowns?'

'Wow,' said Sir Lancelot, Susan and Fissure.

'Wow indeed,' said Morgan le Fey. 'You know what? I reckon if the Princess Floridian is that keen to get Excalibur, you could get her to give you the ruby.'

'But what about the sausage?' said Fissure. 'It's a blood sausage.'

'Are you crazy?' said Sir Lancelot. 'You would rather have a sausage instead of a priceless ruby?'

'It is a blood sausage,' said Fissure.

'I can see his point,' said Fenestra.

'Maybe you could get her to give you both,' Morgan le Fey suggested.

'I'd rather have another sausage,' said Fissure.

'By the way,' said Sir Lancelot, 'what exactly is a sausage?'

'Well,' said the young vampire, 'they are a brilliant

new invention where they get a bit of a dead animal's stomach and stuff it with chopped-up bits of another dead animal mixed up with stuff like fat and blood and then they boil them.'

'And what do they do with them then?' said Sir Lancelot. 'Are they some sort of weapon?'

'No, they eat them.'

'Don't be ridiculous.'

'It's true, my lord,' said Morgan le Fey. 'I have eaten them myself. My brother, the King, adores them and has a sausage banquet on the first Saturday of every month.'

Sir Lancelot looked green. He wondered if the fly-blown giblet curries he eaten on his crusades in strange far-off lands hadn't been so bad after all. He had seen the stomachs of dead animals. They were not the sort of thing you'd want to put into your own stomach. It had made him wonder if it was possible to exist by eating no more than fruit and vegetables and tofu, but had tasted tofu and decided against it.

The brave knight was an old-fashioned sort of person. Sausages might be all right for young people, but he would stick to the traditional dead cow and

163

boiled vegetables. Besides, he was sure sausages were just a passing fad like donkey painting and underwater jousting. A year from now they'd be forgotten like the other new fad of boiling up dried leaves and drinking them. All these trendy new food fads were simply ridiculous.

'Before you know it,' he said, 'people will be roasting beans and grinding them into dust and drinking that.'

'Umm, I think they already do that in far-off lands,' said Morgan le Fey.

'Thank goodness they're far off,' said Sir Lancelot. 'So what is your plan? Shall we gather some guards and go up and arrest them?'

'We could,' said Morgan le Fey, 'but I think they would know we were on our way before we get there, and don't forget they have the young dragon with them. They could simply climb on its back and fly out of the window.'

'The boy and the girl could,' said Fissure. 'If potato boy climbed on the dragon's back it wouldn't get off the ground, and anyway, he's too fat to get out of the window.'

'Oh, they'd just leave him behind,' said Morgan le Fey. 'No, we need to be subtler than that. We need to lure them to one of the islands and trap them there.'

'I could tell them where the island with Excalibur is and take them there,' said Fissure.

'That's not as simple as it sounds,' said Fenestra.

'I thought you said you knew which island the sword is on?' said Morgan le Fey.

'Well, sort of. You see, there are quite a few islands with swords on, in particular the famous Island of Swords,' the vampire explained. 'Then there's the Island of More Swords and the Island of Some Different Swords and the . . .'[49]

'So isn't there an island called the Island of Excalibur?'

'Yes, of course there is, but all the names are a bit pointless really. I mean, it's not like there's a sign on each island saying, "This is the Island of So and So",' said Fenestra. 'Even the Island of So and So hasn't got a sign saying that. In fact there is only one island with a sign on it and that is the Island With No Name.

---

[49] *Of course this isn't even counting the seven Islands of Little Trees That Look Exactly Like Swords.*

'And of course,' the vampire continued, 'as you know most of the islands move around a lot.'

'So you don't know which island has Excalibur on it?'

'Oh yes, we all know which one it is.'

'So how do you find it?'

'It's a process of elimination.'

'Elimination?'

'Yes. For example the Island of Excalibur has a tree on it.'

'Oh that's really helpful,' said Morgan le Fey. 'There are over three hundred islands and they've all got trees on them.'

'Except for the treeless islands,' said the vampire.

'And how many of them are there?'

'One.'

'Brilliant.'

'There are no castles on the island.'

'And how many are there that do have a castle?'

'Fourteen.'

'Wonderful,' said Morgan le Fey. 'So we know there are more than three hundred islands, but not how many more, but we do know that Excalibur is

not on fifteen of them.'

'Exactly,' said the vampire. 'And you can discount the underwater islands.'

'I think if they're underwater, they are not exactly islands.'

'Right. Well, there is a family of donkeys living there.'

'Ah, now that must cut it down quite a bit,' said Sir Lancelot.

'Indeed it does. There are only eighty-five islands that are inhabited by donkeys, though the number does change.'

'How?'

'Well, donkeys can be quite bad-tempered, so they are forever arguing and swimming off to other islands that may or may not already have donkeys on them,' said the vampire.

'OK, so we've cut the number of possible islands down to eighty-five, give or take an unknown and constantly changing number?' said Morgan le Fey.

'Exactly!'

'Anything else special that will eliminate some more?'

'Oh yes,' said the vampire. 'The Island of Excalibur is home to a very rare flower that only grows in one other place.'

'So the list is down to two?'

'It is,' said the vampire. 'The Island of Excalibur and The Spare Island of Excalibur.'

'Spare?'

'Well, surely you don't think something as important and priceless as Excalibur, The Sword That Conquers All Other Swords And Kicks Dirt In Their Faces, wouldn't have a backup in case the original got broken?'

'But if it is the sword that conquers all other swords, how can it get broken?' said Morgan le Fey.

'I hadn't thought of that,' said the vampire.

'OK. We'll worry about that later. In the meantime, what does this flower look like?'

'It is incredibly beautiful,' said the vampire, 'a shade of blue so perfect that it can bring grown men to their knees with a big wet patch in their tights. It only flowers for fifteen minutes at midnight on midsummer's eve and then it sleeps until the next midsummer's eve. Or so I've been told.'

'So you haven't actually seen it?'

'No.'

'Right.'

'But I do know someone who says they know someone who has.'

'What a bit of luck,' said Sir Lancelot. 'For is not tonight midsummer's eve?'

It was.

Fenestra agreed to go back and get all her relatives to fly out across the lake as night fell to search for the two islands with their brilliant blue flowers. When they found them, they were to land and send a message back by sonar with its location.

'Then we will hide on the islands while Fissure goes back to the bandits and leads them to the island,' said Morgan le Fey.

'How will I know which is the Island of Excalibur and which island is the Spare Island of Excalibur?' said the young vampire.

'You won't,' said Fenestra. 'Only one person will know that and that will be the One True King of Avalon and even he won't know until he pulls the One True Excalibur out of the rock.'

'What happens if he chooses the wrong one?'

'No one really knows,' said the vulture, 'but the soothsayers have been saying all sort of scary sooths about violent storms and the end of the world and pimples, but then you know what soothsayers are like.'

'So I'll just lead them to either island, shall I?' said Fissure.

'Haven't got any choice, have you?' said Morgan le Fey. 'I mean, either island is either island or not, isn't it?'

Fissure flew back to the tower where Brat and his cronies were waiting.

'I have spoken to my aunt and she says that tonight the island where Excalibur is will be revealed,' he said.

'Tonight? Tonight?' said Princess Floridian. 'That's a bit suspicious, isn't it? Here we are looking for the sword and by an amazing coincidence tonight is the very night it's going to be revealed.'

'Well, tonight is midsummer's eve,' said Fissure. 'That's when the flowers open up.'

'Flowers, what flowers?' said the Princess. 'I don't like it. It sounds like a trap.'

'Fair enough,' said Fissure. 'I'll go home then.'

'No, no,' said the Princess. 'Here, have a bit of sausage.'

'No, thanks,' said Fissure. 'I've gone off the idea of sausage. I think being a spy is worth a lot more than a sausage.'

'Oh yes? Like what?'

'Well,' said the young vampire. 'Correct me if I'm wrong, but all that pretending you weren't really interested in Excalibur and were just looking for a friend was a load of old garbage, wasn't it? You are totally obsessed with the sword and the invincible power it gives to its owner, aren't you?'

'Umm, no, er,' said the Princess.

She was thrown completely off guard by Fissure. She had thought he was just a stupid gullible flying bird-creature with pointy teeth.

'If I'm wrong, just say so,' said the vampire, 'and I'll leave.'

'No, no, don't go,' said the Princess.

She went over to the window where Fissure was sitting on the sill and spoke in a low voice so the others couldn't hear her.

'Why don't you and I become partners,' she whispered. 'You seem like a smart boy, not like these idiots I'm stuck here with.'

'Go on.'

'That idiot Brat, who managed to get thrown off the throne, thinks he is the rightful owner of Excalibur. He thinks he can pull it out of the stone and then reclaim Avalon.'

'And?'

'Well, maybe he can,' said Princess Floridian. 'So if we work together, we can wait until he has freed the sword and then overpower him and kill him. Then we can take over Avalon.'

'What about potato boy?'

'He can't even fit through the window, never mind sit on the dragon's back. I wouldn't worry about him.'

'And the dragon?'

'He'll do as he's told,' said the Princess. 'So, are you up for it?'

'All right, but you've still got to pay me,' said Fissure. 'I mean, how do I know you won't try and kill me too?'

'What do you want?'

'The ruby.'

'Ruby, what ruby?'

'Hey, us vampires know everything,' said Fissure, hoping the Princess wouldn't make him prove it. 'You give me the ruby and I will lead you to the Island of Excalibur this very night.'

'Do you know how much it's worth?' said the Princess.

'Yes, less than a tenth of a quarter of half a percent of the wealth that Excalibur could bring you.'

'But...'

'I've had enough of this,' said the boy who would one day become King of the Vampires. 'You're too indecisive. I'm off.'

'No, no, no,' cried the Princess. 'I'll give you the ruby.'

'Show me it,' said Fissure.

The Princess reached into her dress and took the stone out from its secret pocket.

'As soon as we have Excalibur, it will be yours.'

'No. Once you have the sword, you could kill me and keep everything. I want the stone now.'

'But what guarantee do I have that you'll will come back tonight and lead me to the island?'

'None at all,' said Fissure. 'You'll just have to take that risk.'

'But . . .'

'I can see you are torn,' said Fissure, licking his fangs. 'So let's forget the whole thing.'

The Princess handed the ruby to Fissure.

'I will return at midnight,' he said and flew back across the castle to Morgan le Fey and Sir Lancelot.

The Princess and the fearless knight were very impressed when Fissure showed them the ruby. Not so much his auntie Fenestra.

'What are you going to do with that then?' she said.

'Umm, er,' said Fissure, 'but it's worth ten million gold crowns.'

'And what would you do with ten million gold crowns?'

'Umm, er, umm. I could buy . . . umm. How much do blood sausages cost?'

'Stupid boy,' said Fenestra.

Fissure flew over to the vampire tower and put the ruby in his toy box along with his rabbit's heart football and his dried kitten slippers.

'I think it's time we sent for your brother,' said Sir Lancelot. 'I think he should know what's going on.'

'You're right,' Morgan le Fey agreed, 'Merlin too. His experience will guide us. After all, he guided my father to victory through several wars so this will be simple by comparison. My instinct is to get a few soldiers, grab them all and kill them. Merlin, no doubt, will take a more subtle approach that will probably be wiser.'

Morgan le Fey sent for her brother and the old wizard and told them what was happening.

'Fetch King Kasterwheel too,' said Morgan le Fey, 'that he may be reunited with his daughter, though I don't know that he will want her back.'

'Excellent,' said Merlin. 'This will be the perfect opportunity to kill lots of birds with one stone.'

'Indeed,' said Morgan le Fey. 'We'll capture the

wretched runaways and my beloved brother can claim Excalibur. This will be a night for the history books, a night that will become a legend.'

Bit like you, gorgeous, she thought as she glanced at Sir Lancelot, a knight who was already a legend.

'Maybe not just one stone, but a lot of stones and some very pointy weapons too,' said the wizard.

'Now you are talking my kind of language,' said Lancelot and he sent for four boatloads of heavily armed soldiers.

As midnight approached, everyone went down to the water's edge and waited for a signal from the vampires, who were now floating above the islands, that the rare and beautiful flower had opened.

'By the way, my child,' said Merlin, 'when all this is over, you must tell me how you can get the vampires to do your bidding.'

Morgan le Fey was surprised and delighted that the old wizard had no inkling of her relationship with Fenestra.

It must be the only thing in all of Camelot that he knows nothing about, she smiled to herself. *Unless, of course, he's bluffing and playing a game.*

But he wasn't.

He knew nothing of the friendship between the Princess and the vampires. Had he done so, he would have moved heaven and earth to stop it. A princess with a small army of vampire bats would be too formidable a threat for him to deal with.

For their part, the vampires did not like Merlin. In common with nearly every human, they did not trust him.

Meanwhile, above the lake all the vampires glided back and forth across the lake watching for the magic moment. Every single vampire was there, even the ancient Lucestays. As she was completely blind, it had been cruel and pointless waking the ancient bat, but that's the sort of thing vampires do.

'Oh no,' said Morgan le Fey, 'I think it's beginning to rain.'

But it wasn't. Lucestays the Ancient who was also Lucestays the Incontinent had just flown overhead.

The first sonar signal came in a few minutes after midnight followed three minutes later by the second. Merlin waved his special weather-controlling wand and a layer of thick clouds covered the moon as the

177

four boats rowed silently towards the islands.

As soon as they had landed and everyone had hidden behind a tree or a sleeping donkey,[50] small fires was lit on each island to act as beacons and Fissure flew back up to the tower where Brat, Bloat and Princess Floridian were waiting for him.

Scraper was waiting too, but he hadn't the faintest idea what he was waiting for, which was basically the story of his whole life. At least it meant that when Brat and the Princess flew off on Bloat's back leaving him behind, he wouldn't be too upset.

'I have a really, really important job for you,' Brat told him as they prepared to leave.

'A spy has told me that someone is coming to

---

[50] *These were not the donkeys that lived on the other islands, but the four donkeys that had belonged to Armoire the Donkey Lifter. Three had swum there when they had been thrown into the lake and the fourth had flown, or rather been thrown, straight there when the bamboo tower had collapsed.*

steal the door handle to this very room. While we are out, you must guard the handle with your life. OK?'

'Are they go to steal this handle on the inside of the door?' said Scraper, 'or the one on the outside.'

'Both.'

'Can I have an assistant then?'

'No, just leave the door half-open so you can watch both handles at once,' said the Princess.

Brat and Princess Floridian climbed onto Bloat's back and followed Fissure out of the window. They flew down through the dark night towards the lake where the two fires twinkled like a pair of eyes.

'Which one's got the sword?' Princess Floridian shouted.

'I don't know,' Fissure called back.

He hovered in the air until Bloat caught up with him.

'That's ridiculous,' said the Princess.

'No one knows,' said the young vampire, 'but there's only two to choose from. If it's not one, it'll be the other.'

He landed by the nearest fire while the Princess told Bloat to land on the other island fifty metres away.

The islands were identical down to the last blade of grass so there was no way of knowing which one held the true Excalibur.

'This has all been too easy,' she said. 'I think it could be a trap.'

Naturally, as soon as the flowers had been spotted, Sir Lancelot had hidden soldiers on the two islands. They now emerged from the darkness and threw a large net over the arrivals, making it impossible for the young dragon to fly off.

'So this is the right island then,' said Princess Floridian.

'Not necessarily,' said Sir Lancelot, stepping forward and drawing his sword. 'The young vampire was telling the truth when he said no one knows which of the twin islands holds the true Excalibur.'

'Are you the great Sir Lancelot?' said Princess Floridian.

'I am indeed.'

'Oh praise be,' said the Princess, falling off Bloat's back in a faint. 'Good knight, I have been grossly mistreated, kidnapped and dragged away from my beloved father by this evil boy and his dragon. If you

will slay them and rescue me, I am sure my father will reward you handsomely and, dare I say it, give you my hand in marriage.'

'Is that so, my lady?'

'It is indeed, oh great and noble knight.'

Princess Floridian grabbed a handful of mud and, turning away, rubbed it into her hair and all over her face.

'Can you not see, my lord, how I have been maltreated?' the Princess continued. 'I have been thrown in mud and covered in dragon's spit and had nasty pointy bits of grass poked up my pert yet dainty nose.'

'Well, well,' said Sir Lancelot. 'We can't have your legendary beauty all muddy and bespoiled, can we?'

He beckoned two soldiers who pulled Princess Floridian out from the net and threw her in the lake. The soldiers were seasoned campaigners. They had travelled the world serving the great Sir Lancelot on his quests, crusades and adventures. They had seen it all and they had heard it all. Yet that night they learned seventeen new swear words that outdid the greatest obscenities they had ever heard. The words were made

all the more shocking as they came from the mouth of a Princess so beautiful that one would hardly imagine butter melting there.

But in Princess Floridian's mouth butter would not merely melt, it would turn rancid, boil and froth and be spat out as scalding acid.

'You think, my child, that you and your little friends were unobserved?' said Merlin, emerging from the shadows. 'We have seen your every move.'

'You will all die, you vile [*insert seventeen of your favourite disgusting swearwords here*] scum!' the Princess screamed. 'When I claim Excalibur I will shred you into human coleslaw.'

'Claim? Claim?' said Merlin. 'You think you are the rightful owner of the enchanted sword?'

'Of course I am, moron. Do you think my kidnapping and all that which has brought me here was just an accident?'

'No, no accident,' said the wizard. 'More of a series of clumsy, stupid mistakes.'

'I will prove it,' sneered the Princess. 'I will pull the sword from the stone.'

'Well, yes indeed,' said Merlin. 'That would prove

it beyond doubt.'

Before she could climb out of the lake, there was an enormous commotion behind her. The water thrashed about in a wild frenzy, bringing whatever was causing the thrashing closer and closer until it was barely thirty feet away.

'The Great Olm has decided your fate, my dear,' said Merlin.

Sir Lancelot and the two soldiers ran towards the water's edge. Merlin held up his hands to stop them. Lightning sprang from his fingertips and shot up into the clouds. A look of sheer terror came into Princess Floridian's eyes. The screaming, angry she-devil was transformed back into a little girl. Brat and Bloat struggled to get out of the net, but only succeeded in tangling themselves up more. Bloat's fire-breathing was rubbish at the best of times and not only that, the net was made of asbestos which is fireproof. Brat was not fireproof and got a few nasty burns.

'Do not enter the water,' said Merlin to Sir Lancelot. 'The Enchanted Lake has spoken and must not be questioned.'

'I didn't know the lake was enchanted,' said

Morgan le Fey.

'Oh yes, my lady. It overflows with enchantosity,' said the wizard. 'The very water itself is alive.'

'Actually, it isn't,' he whispered, 'I'm just screwing around with the Princess's mind.'

'But won't the olms get her?'

'I think you will see that it is not an olm that approaches,' said Merlin. 'Olms are terrified of midsummer's eve and stay hidden in the depths until it has passed.'

He was right. The splashing got closer and more chaotic and a huge blunt head emerged from the water.

'I will save you, my lady,' it shouted.

It was Scraper.

He picked up the Princess and waded ashore.

'DROP IT!' Merlin shouted.

The wet, scared, but still angry and defiant Princess Floridian fell on the grass, muttering and cursing.

'Right, your highness, there is the stone. There is the mighty sword which may or may not be Excalibur,' said Merlin. 'Claim your birthright.'

'You will so regret this, you stupid old fool,'

sneered Princess Floridian.

She got to her feet, walked over the sword and, taking the hilt in both hands, pulled as hard as she could.

Nothing happened.

'It seems to be stuck,' she said. 'It's probably gone rusty with sitting here so long.'

'It is rust-proof, my lady,' said Merlin, 'made of the finest stainless steel.'

'Well, it's stuck,' said the Princess, going red in the face.

'I think that proves that you are not the chosen one,' said Sir Lancelot.

'Don't be stupid, of course I am. I need an unguent to free the blade. I need a vial of Ye WD42.'[51]

'It will make no difference, my lady.'

Scraper took hold of the great sword's hilt and pulled with all his might.

Slowly the great sword lifted into the air.

The trouble was, so did the huge rock it was

---

[51] *WD42 – Wizards' De-Ruster. The 42 is the number of times it had been used to free various enchanted swords, daggers and lances from various enchanted rocks, stones and dead persons.*

trapped in. Scraper held it above his head and was about to speak when his arms gave way and the three-ton rock flattened him and his beloved bucket. His mouth, still open wide, did not utter a sound on account of him being overcome with dead.

Princess Floridian stood rooted to the spot. The rock had missed her by inches. She reached out and touched the hilt of the sword, but it didn't move.

'That went well, I thought,' said Merlin, unable to hide a grin.

'One more test,' he added. 'Fetch the evil boy. Let him try. If he is the true King, the sword will come free, and if this is the true sword we shall fall at his feet. If it does come free and it is not the true sword we will not fall at his feet. Instead we will clear up the bits.'

Brat was hauled out of the net and led to the sword. He had heard rumours that pulling the fake Excalibur would lead the puller to a fate worse than death[52] and was scared.

'I don't want to,' he said.

'But I thought you said you were the one true

---

[52] *See the back of this book for a lovely selection of fates worse than death.*

186

King of Camelot,' said Morgan le Fey. 'Pull Excalibur from the stone and prove it. Succeed and we shall acknowledge you as our supreme leader, knowing that you were right all along.'

'I don't want to,' he said. 'I've decided I don't want to be King anymore.'

'So you would rather go back to the kitchens, would you?'

'I, er . . .'

'I am sure the Cook would be delighted to see you,' Morgan le Fey laughed.

'No, but, I mean, I . . .' said Brat and he fell on his knees.

'You're pathetic,' sneered Princess Floridian.

She grabbed the scruff of the boy's neck, hauled him to his feet and wrapped his arms round the sword.

'Pull, you little scumbag.'

Brat tried to push, but the Princess, who was stronger than he was, wrapped her hands over his and pulled.

The Princess thought she could feel the sword begin to move. It was the slightest tremor, but there definitely was something. She pulled harder and the

movement grew stronger, but it was not the sword leaving the stone. It was the ground beneath their feet.

The Princess let go of Brat's hands and leapt back.

The ground opened and swallowed Brat. Revolting noises came from the hole, along with smoke and a terrible smell of burnt rags and sulphur.

Obviously this was not the true Excalibur.

The ground shook again and what can only be described as a really sticky phlegm-filled cough came out of the centre of the earth, followed by a slightly toasted small boy.

Then the ground closed again.

'Way to go, Mother Nature,' said Morgan le Fey.

Brat, who was naked apart from a thin coating of soot, lay curled up in the grass smoking[53] and whimpering.

'Well, well, the fearless warrior who will take over the world has returned from the very centre of the earth,' said Morgan le Fey, rolling him over with her foot.

Everyone except Princess Floridian fell about

---

[53] *As in having been on fire, not smoking a cigarette. This was long before the idea of rolling up some dried weeds, setting fire to them and putting them in your mouth had been thought of.*

laughing. Brat's humiliation was complete. The Princess helped him to his feet. It wasn't that she felt sorry for him or even liked him, but the two of them were seen by everyone as two parts of the same pathetic rebellion, so his defeat reflected on her too. Though, being the selfish, resourceful girl she was, she was sure she would be able to turn the situation to her advantage.

Meanwhile, on the other island, King Arthur and the rest of the soldiers waited for news. No one knew what might happen if someone pulled out the wrong sword. There were all the rumours, of course, hundreds of them. The most popular were:

- Nothing.
- Whoever was holding the sword would be turned into:
  - A plate of pickled herrings.

- ▸ An incomplete collection of Belgian postage stamps.[54]
- ▸ Tartan socks.[55]
- ▸ A small jellyfish wearing ballet shoes.
- ▸ A chimney.
- ▸ Four metres of pink taffeta.
- The entire world would tip up a bit which, considering everyone thought the world was flat in those days, would mean most of the seas would fall off. There would be a lot of fish to eat for a while, but all the whales would be floating around in space and might come crashing to earth at any time.[56]
- Tears before bedtime.
- Something else.
- Tears during and after bedtime too.
- It's not my turn to do the washing up.[57]

---

[54] *This was a very strange yet popular belief, because no country was due to invent a postal system for hundreds of years.*

[55] *See footnote 34 – same timescale.*

[56] *One Avalon entrepreneur made a nice living for a brief period by selling reinforced Anti-Whale Hats.*

[57] *Oops, not sure how that got in there.*

The young King stared at the sword in the stone and it was all he could do to stop himself grabbing hold of it. His fingers twitched. The anticipation was killing him. He began to walk over to the stone.

'Sire, I know what you are thinking,' said Lancebit, Sir Lancelot's second in command,[58] placing himself between Arthur and the maybe sword. 'I would be tempted too, but please, sire, I beg of you, do not touch the sword until we get news. If you never own the true sword, you will still be the greatest King Camelot has ever had.'

He ordered his men to form a circle around the rock, though everyone knew that if the King did decide to go for the sword, no one would dare stop him.

'We do not have long to wait, sire,' said the general. 'I think I hear a boat approaching from the other island.'

'I thought *this* was the other island,' said King Arthur.

'Yes, but only if you are on the other island, sire. To us this is *the* island and the other island is the other island.'

---

[58]   *Top soldier dude.*

191

'Right.'

The boat arrived, bringing everyone from the island that was not the one King Arthur was on.

'This is the true stone,' said Merlin. 'Your majesty, your destiny awaits you. You may claim Excalibur.'

One of the soldiers, who always carried a drum for special occasions, beat out a great drum roll as the young King, who no one doubted was the actual one and only true King of Avalon,[59] approached the sword.

He grasped the hilt in his light hands and pulled.

The crowd waited in silence and then . . .

Nothing happened.

'Just kidding,' Arthur laughed and the sword slid free.

'Phew,' said everyone.

They breathed a huge collective sigh of relief followed by a great cheer.

Then everyone fell silent and looked at the King.

---

[59] *Even Brat knew that Arthur was the real king, though he would never admit it. Princess Floridian had always known it, but figured it was worth trying to get hold of Excalibur anyway. She didn't so much want to do lots of killing with it, as sell it for an unimaginable amount of money.*

It is at moments like these that the whole world is filled with love and forgiveness. Brat, seeing his opportunity to save his skin, fell at the King's feet.

'Oh sire,' he whined, 'I have been a vain and selfish boy. I have caused disarray and unhappiness, but now I see the error of my ways and wish to serve you.'

King Arthur, full of wisdom and nobility way beyond his young years, looked down at the pathetic figure grovelling before him. The boy, still naked apart from his coating of soot and a pink sock Princess Floridian had given him, reminded Arthur of how he himself had looked not so many weeks before when he had been a kitchen boy and Brat had been the King. Now the wretched child was barely distinguishable from the mud in which he slithered around.[60]

'I will devote the rest of my life to your great majestiness and stand at your side ready to vanquish anyone who should threaten you,' Brat snivelled.

Then everyone fell even more silent and looked at the King some more.

---

[60] *Brat was slithering because it had started raining, not your normal type of rain, but very localised rain from one of Merlin's spells that made it rain only on Brat and Princess Floridian.*

193

Arthur lowered Excalibur to the ground and looked down at Brat. An extremely regal light came into his wonderful blue eyes.

'Yeah, right,' he said. 'Take him back to the kitchens.'

Everyone breathed a second collective sigh of relief followed by a great cheer.

'Oh, and this time,' King Arthur continued, 'put some leg irons on him.'

Then it was Princess Floridian's turn to grovel.

'Oh great and wise King,' she began, 'your decision shows the true wonderfulosity of your cleverness and wisefulness. I thank you for punishing my kidnapper, the evil boy who snatched me away from the arms of my beloved father and forced me into a life of highwaypersonness and not washing. My great and wonderful father, who loves me more than life itself, will reward you with great rewardy stuff. He will probably give you my hand in marriage too and happy would I be were he to do so, to be the wife of such a wise and handsome living god.'

King Kasterwheel, who had been standing in the shadows since arriving on the island, now came

forward. His daughter had no idea he knew she had killed her mother so his reaction was totally not what she had been expecting.

'Actually, I will not pay any reward to get you back,' said King Kasterwheel. 'Though I'd be only too happy to reward my young friend King Arthur if he will keep you here. I'm sure the leg irons he gave the nasty little boy will not be the only pair in Camelot. And as for marriage, I will indeed give you to be someone's bride, but only on one condition.'

'Oh father, anything to regain your love,' Princess Floridian lied. 'What is the condition? Just tell me and I will agree.'

'Agreeing has nothing to do with it. You have no choice in the matter,' said King Kasterwheel. 'The condition is that you are going to become the bride of your ally, the vile kitchen boy. Of course, neither of you are old enough to get married yet, so I suggest you are both sent to the castle kitchens to scrub the floors until you are.'

'Mrs Floridian Brat,' said Morgan le Fey. 'What a lovely name.'

'Indeed,' said King Kasterwheel. 'And I hereby

disinherit you and take back your title of Princess. You may keep your pink socks.'

'Oh father,' Princess Floridian cried. 'I see it now. You are merely playing with my emotions to tease me. Obviously you are not serious.'

'Why do you say that, daughter?' said the King.

'The idea of making me, a royal Princess of the purest regal-type blood, marry a lowly peasant, is obviously a joke. No loving father would ever dream of such a thing.'

'Well, you see the thing is,' said King Kasterwheel, 'I am not a loving father. I am an old fool who has been taken in by his nasty daughter for far too long. I know what you did to your mother. The old clown confessed it all before he died. So yes, you are right, I would never dream of such a thing for I am not dreaming. I am wide awake. You are henceforth betrothed to the kitchen boy and may he beat you every day and dress you in cabbage leaves and give you fifteen nasty, whining little children with terrible skin conditions and noses that will never stop running.'

There was a slight pause followed by a great cheer. Justice had been done in a just and fitting way.

Or had it?

Merlin wondered about the wisdom of joining the two evil beings together, especially having them live in Camelot itself.

It could end in tears, he thought. *The joining together with chains is good. The joining together in marriage, maybe not so great.*

Time Dragson

As everyone got back into the two boats to go back to the castle, a single pathetic voice drifted across the water.

'Hello,' it cried. 'Is there anyone there?'

'Did you hear something?' said Morgan le Fey as they rowed away.

'Do you mean a weak little voice saying, "Hello, is there anyone there?"' said King Arthur.

'Yes.'

'No.'

'Me neither.'

The pathetic voice belonged to the one being they had left behind on the other island. Bloat was still trapped under the fire-proof net and the more he struggled, the more entangled he became. He hadn't been forgotten, but it was generally agreed, especially by his parents, who had been sent for to reclaim their errant son, that he was a gullible and not very bright young dragon who, unlike Princess Floridian and Brat, was not an evil creature. He had been a naughty boy and needed to be taught a lesson.

'I think,' said his father, Spikeweed, King of the

Dragons, 'that we'll leave him there for a few days. It's raining, so if he opens his mouth he'll have enough to drink and a couple of days without food will certainly not do him any harm.'

'But he is my little boy,' said his mother, Primrose. 'I can't bear the idea of him being all alone out there on that island.'

'He isn't alone,' said Spikeweed. 'He's got the flattened remains of potato boy to keep him company and the rats and cockroaches that will be eating potato boy.'

The bits of Scraper that were sticking out from under the big rock were not only company, they were breakfast, lunch and dinner. Bloat might not have been able to free himself from the net to fly away, but he did manage to wriggle around enough to nibble away at the bits of Scraper he could see.

Of course, this meant that by the time his father went to free him, he had actually put on weight, not lost it.

'Still,' said Spikeweed, 'It's good to see you doing some recycling.'

When they got back to the Valley of the Dragons, Bloat turned over a new leaf. Actually he was so keen

to make a new start, he turned over an entire tree and three bushes, a total of seventeen thousand, five hundred and seventy-seven new leaves. Actually less than a thousand of the leaves were new, the rest had been there for ages. He changed his name to Ambrose and began pressing flowers, which normally requires the one thing dragons do not have – thumbs – but Ambrose developed a system that most flower-pressing dragons still use to this day. He sat on them.[61] The only downside to this was that quite often flowers got stuck to Ambrose's bottom and the sight of a teenage dragon wandering about with a bouquet on his behind meant he got teased a lot.

'I am an artist. I am above such childish humour,' he would say and walk off to the nearest meadow to spend the day writing poetry, another thing that was difficult to do without thumbs. He could make up poems easily enough, but he couldn't write them down. His parents gave him a talking parrot to remember his creations, but it kept getting confused and muddling them up.

---

[61] *Apart from a group of dragons living in the remote pine forests of northern Russia who press flowers by dropping huge brown bears on them.*

For example:

My Love is Like a Red, Red Cockatoo

A poem by Ambrose the Dragon (and Polly)

I sit here in this meadow.
My soul is full of Joy
My heart is full of Love
Polly's a pretty boy.

You are more lovely than a tree
My life, you do fulfil it
I want so much to make you mine.
Polly wants some millet.

To spend my every day with you
Would be my greatest wish
To cherish and to hold you dear
Polly wants a cuttlefish

Ambrose got very few of his poems published apart from a couple in *Ye Parrot Fancyers Gazette* who were very enthusiastic and made him their arts columnist even though he knew nothing at all about columns.

ᛖeanwhile, Brat and Princess Floridian, both shackled round the ankles and thrown into a small boat, were rowed back to shore behind the two main boats by two soldiers.

Ahead of them Arthur stood proudly at the helm of the first boat holding Excalibur high in the air so that everyone waiting on the shore could see it as they approached.

You might think, as did everyone who was watching, that a boy as young and slender as King Arthur would hardly be able to lift a sword as large and magnificent as Excalibur, but as it had shown by refusing to leave the enchanted rock for anyone but the King, the sword itself was filled with magic. Thus, for Arthur it became as light as a feather.

Crouched together in the back of their small boat, Princess Floridian and Brat seethed with anger. This was the lowest point of their lives and they consoled themselves with that fact.

'No matter what happens from now on,' said Brat, 'nothing can be worse than today has been.'

'Maybe, but that is no consolation,' said the

Princess. 'I want revenge. I want super-enemy-crippling-totally-overwhelming-completely-annihilating revenge. I want to grind all of them into tiny little piles of dust and for them to know who did it and I want them to wish they were all dead, but they're not. They're all just screaming in pain and begging over and over again for us to stop the pain, but it won't ever stop because I want them to know forever they are the losers and we won.'

'Yeah,' said Brat. 'All that what you said. I want that too.'

'First of all we need to escape,' said the Princess. 'And we need to do it before they get us locked down in the kitchens.'

She threw herself on her back and began groaning and wailing in pain.

'What's the matter?' said Brat.

'What's the matter?' said the two soldiers who had stopped rowing and come to see.

'I think I am dying,' Princess Floridian cried. 'A pain more terrible than death is eating me all up.'

'Where?' said Soldier Number One.

The Princess arched her back and screamed.

'I am possessed by an evil spirit,' she cried. 'It possessed me many weeks ago and now we are to be enslaved in the dungeons of Camelot, it is trying to kill me so it can escape before we are locked up.'

'Was it the evil spirit that turned you wicked?' said Soldier Number Two.

Brilliant, thought the Princess.

'It was. It was,' she cried. 'Please help me, good sir, to drive it out before it kills me.'

'What can we do?' said the soldiers.

'I fear it is too late,' the Princess sobbed.

'Oh no, your highness,' said Soldier Number One. 'There must be something we can do.'

'Pull the boat ashore on the nearest island,' said the Princess. 'And lay me on soft grass that I may die close to the earth and not adrift in a cursed boat.'

The two soldiers rowed towards a small island which was wonderfully conveniently hidden from the two boats ahead by another bigger island. As one of the soldiers bent down to lay the Princess on the ground, she threw her legs over his head and crossed her feet, pulling the chain on her shackles around his neck.

'My lady,' said the soldier, 'take care or you may choke me.'

'Oh really,' said Princess Floridian. 'What, like this?'

Brat, who had finally realised that the Princess was not actually possessed by an evil spirit, though he did believe in that sort of thing, threw himself at the second soldier, who tripped and fell in the lake. The Princess, having killed her soldier, was about to leap into the water to strangle the other one too when the water frothed and boiled and the very hungry Giant Olm saved her the trouble.

'Wow,' said Brat. 'You are amazing. I can't believe I'm going to marry you.'

'I wouldn't count on that happening,' said the Princess.

They pulled the boat further ashore and hid it under a bush before throwing the first soldier into the water, where the Giant Olm's three hungry children disposed of him.

'The first thing we need to do is get these shackles off our ankles,' said the Princess. 'Then we will use the boat to make our escape down the river.'

'What river?'

'Do you not know that at the far end of Camelot's lake there is a river that flows many miles through Avalon until it reaches the sea?'

'Well actually,' said Brat, 'I didn't even know the lake had a far end. Until I escaped from the kitchens, I had never been anywhere except Camelot where I was taken as a newborn baby and swapped with King Arthur. When I was the King, I was having too great a time to want to go anywhere else and when I was thrown into the kitchens I was not allowed outside at all until Scraper helped me escape.'

The Princess was right, though, at the far end of the lake, a river – the River Stycks – led to the sea. It was no ordinary river that anyone could simply sail up and possibly invade Camelot. It was an enchanted river with a magical non-return valve invented by Merlin that only allowed boats to travel away from the lake, not towards it. Strange half-visible River Sprites guarded it in case invaders came with their own wizards who could undo Merlin's spell, but none of this was a problem to the two runaways as they wanted to leave, not invade.

'Not yet anyway,' said Princess Floridian. 'We'll do the invading later. First we need to get away and gather our forces.'

'Yeah,' said Brat. 'Gather our forces.'

But first they needed to break free of their chains. They could, of course, row the boat without breaking their bonds, but as the Princess pointed out, if they were followed and forced to abandon their boat and flee overland, only being able to take tiny baby steps could possibly be a bit of a drawback.

'You know, like we would be drawn back to the castle dungeons.'

'We need a blacksmith,' said Brat.

'Indeed.'

The island they were on was little more than a big rock. It had a small patch of grass, two bushes, a tree, a tiny beach made of four hundred and thirty-seven pebbles and an empty bottle that had washed up on the beach. It did not have a blacksmith's shop, just a secondhand coracle shop that was closed.

However, a short row away was the Island of Blacksmiths where all the armour was made.

'We need to get there before anyone realises we

210

are missing,' said the Princess as they pushed the boat into the water.

'Do you think we should go and rescue Bloat?' said Brat.

'No, he's been pretty useless.'

'I know, but I just thought it might be handy to have a dragon with us.'

'Forget him,' said the Princess. 'When we've escaped, we'll get a better one. We'll get a grown-up one that doesn't burn its toes every time it breathes fire and definitely one that doesn't keep setting everyone's farts alight.'

Brat's eyes watered when he remembered that.

'Hello, hello, children, what have we got here?' said the first blacksmith when they reached the Island of Blacksmiths.

'Umm . . .' the Princess began.

'Now listen to me, my good man. We were at a party, you know, one of those wonderful parties for Lords and Ladies and royal people like us, well, no, of course you wouldn't know. Well, anyway, everyone thought it would be a jolly super joke to put shackles on each other and pretend we were dangerous criminals,'

211

said Brat in one of those stupid voices people who think they are very important use,[62] 'and then some idiot chappie was sitting on the toilet and the keys fell out of their pocket, don'tcha know, and so our dear mother sent us here to see you to cut these sort of shackly things off.'

Princess Floridian stared at the young boy in admiration. Up to that point she had thought he was a very great number of groats short of a quite small gold coin, but suddenly he seemed a lot brighter.

'See those lights in the distance,' Brat continued, pointing towards the two boats that were taking King Arthur and everyone back to the castle. 'Our parents are in those boats and they are bringing money to pay you with. Well, I *say* bringing money, but of course our mother never touches such filthy stuff. I mean her butler will be here soon with a purse of gold coinage.'

'But they are rowing away from here,' said the blacksmith.

---

[62] *You know, like the Queen of England and, even worse, like people who want you to think they are someone awfully posh and important and not some inbred chinless wonder which, of course, they are.*

'Well, yes, of course, that's because my mother forgot her purse. She grabbed the wrong handbag when we set off and is going back for the right one,' said Brat without pausing for a second's thought.

'Fair enough,' said the blacksmith. 'Fancy dress party was it, you both dressed in muddy clothes like two peasants?'

'Indeed,' said Brat. 'Surely you've heard of the Grand Annual Peasants Ball where us nobles and toffs dress up as peasants and get drunk and do peasanty things?'

'Oh, yes of course,' said the blacksmith, who had heard of no such thing, but didn't want to appear ignorant, 'and all the peasants dress up as toffs and nobles.'

'No they don't,' said Brat. 'That's a completely different ball.'

'So what do the peasants dress up as at this one?'

'Peasants.'

'Could you please remove our shackles immediately?' said Princess Floridian. 'I am due to be presented to our wonderful King Arthur and need to hurry back to the palace.'

'Well, I was thinking it might be a good idea to wait until your mother's man arrives with the money,' said the blacksmith.

'Oh no,' said Brat, 'please don't wait until our parents get here. Our father is in the boat and he will go crazy if he finds out what happened. He thinks we are here to save a poor little puppy that has its head stuck in an iron grating.'

'Well, I'm not sure,' said the blacksmith.

'I will tell my mother there were five puppies and that it took you a very long time and she has to pay you double,' said Brat.

Just to help things along, the Princess began to cry.

'Oh, all right,' said the blacksmith.

It only took five minutes and then the two children were free.

'I see the boats have arrived at Camelot,' said the blacksmith. 'Let us wait until they come back.'

'I have a better idea,' said Brat. 'Why don't we take you back in our boat to the castle, then you won't have to wait so long.'

'Indeed. I'll send my son with you. I have twenty

pairs of steel underpants to make by the morrow,' said the blacksmith. 'Rampart, go with these two to Camelot and collect fifteen groats from their mother.'

'How will I get back again?' said Rampart.

'Because you helped us without our parents finding out,' said Brat, 'we will reward you with this boat. I don't suppose you have a couple of small swords we could borrow for the journey? I hear there are pirates abroad on the lake.'

'Take these,' said the blacksmith, handing them two swords he had made that very morning, 'and you better take these stabbing daggers too, just in case.'

'And maybe a few sandwiches, for we have missed our dinner,' said Brat.

Princess Floridian gazed open-mouthed at her companion. She could not believe how he had changed. One minute he had been the spoilt, petulant eleven-year-old brat he had been named after, and the next he was acting as if he really was a royal Prince and at least ten years older than his true age.

Of course she hadn't known him when he had been the King and used to ordering people around all the time. And boy, had he been bossy then. So he'd

had plenty of practice, but now it was different. Now he seemed to have an air of maturity that he had been completely devoid of as the King. It was hard to say what was bringing this change about. Maybe it was the thought of being shackled in the kitchens that had made him grow up so suddenly or maybe it was the idea of possibly marrying the incredibly beautiful Princess Floridian in a few years' time. Whatever it was, the Princess liked it. She even thought that she might possibly even perhaps maybe consider marrying him in ten years or so, unless she met someone else, which of course was not only possible, but extremely likely considering how gorgeous she was.

Whatever, she thought. *Though methinks you will need a new name from this night on.*

The three of them got back into the boat and began to row towards Camelot. Once they were hidden by another island, Brat ordered Rampart to stop rowing.

'Now here's the thing,' he said. 'We have three choices.'

Rampart, who looked about two years older than Brat and two years younger than Princess Floridian, was

about twice the size of both of them added together. Yet he was the only one of the three of them not holding a sword in one hand and a stabbing dagger in the other.

'Choices?' said Rampart.

'Yes,' said the soon-to-be-renamed Brat. 'We can either invite you to jump overboard and swim for it, or we can set you ashore on that island there, or we can kill you.'

'Can I decide?' said Rampart.

'OK,' said Brat. 'What's it to be?'

'Well, first of all,' said Rampart, 'may I ask you a question?'

'You may.'

'If I was to say I think you may be the two highwaymen that everyone has been talking about, would you say I could be right?'

'You could be.'

'In that case,' said Rampart. 'There is a fourth choice.'

'Which is?'

'I will join you and we will run away together,' said Rampart.

'And where do you suggest we run away to?'

said Princess Floridian. 'The King will have spies and soldiers scouring the whole of Avalon to find us.'

'I would suggest we travel by night and make our escape down the River Stycks that flows many miles through Avalon until it reaches the sea.'

'And know you this river?' said the Princess.

'I do indeed, my lady. For my father and I have travelled down it many time delivering swords and shields and iron underpants to the towns that lie along its route.'

'And why would you want to join us?' said Brat.

'Indeed,' said Rampart. 'Why would I want to leave a life of drudgery in my father's foundry pumping the bellows from dawn to dusk with never a word of thanks and naught but a potato and a sheep's knee for my dinner? Why indeed?'

'Fair enough,' said Brat. 'Welcome, good Rampart.'

'Welcome indeed,' said Princess Floridian. 'We will begin our journey this very night, for I cannot imagine there will be much more time before they all realise we have escaped.'

As she spoke a loud roar rolled across the

water and a giant flame shot up in the air like a great searchlight, telling the runaways that their escape had finally been noticed. Silhouetted in its light, the Vampires of Camelot spread out across the lake searching for the runaways by the light cast by the flame. Rampart pulled in to the nearest island and tore some branches from a large bush, which he wove together over the top of the boat.

'Thus they will think us no more than a fallen tree floating in the water,' he said. 'It's an old smuggler's trick my father taught me when we were carrying contraband turnips downriver to Tintagel.'

'It will mean we can travel in broad daylight too,' he added.

Brat and the Princess knew they had made a good choice allowing the young blacksmith to join them. They had guile and evil cunning, but Rampart was practical. They would have never thought of something as simple as a few branches to disguise their boat. They would have tried to whip up a magic invisibility spell which, considering neither of them were wizards, would have been completely pointless.

'There is one more thing we must do before we

219

leave,' said Princess Floridian.

'Yes?' said Brat.

'Yes, we must give you a new name.'

'I've got one you can use,' said Rampart. 'It's brilliant. I was keeping it for when I have a son of my own, but you can have it, if you like.'

'Are you sure?' said Brat.

'Absolutely. You two have rescued me from a life of mindless monotony. It's the least I can do.'

'Go on then,' said Princess Floridian. 'What is it?'

'Brassica,' said Rampart.

'I love it,' said Brat.

'So do I,' said Princess Floridian. 'And it sounds great if you put Prince or King in front of it.'

'Oh yes. Prince Brassica. I like it,' said Brat who was now Brassica, and he muttered softly to himself: 'King Brassica of Avalon.'

They hacked down three bushes and set them adrift on the water, following in their own disguised boat. All the water in Lake Camelot drifted slowly towards the river, so all they had to do was use the oars now and then to change direction slightly and get up a bit more speed.

HAS THIS EVER HAPPENED TO YOU?

It is early morning in the middle of winter. The temperature is way below freezing. There is thick ice covering the lake around Camelot and you have to go off to fight a great battle. Can you imagine how cold your suit of armour is on this harsh morning? It is so cold that the steel will stick to your skin and tear it away in bloody strips.

Fear not, BRAVE KNIGHT. Help is at hand.

THE LORD ANORAX
AMAZING ARMOUR WARMER
IS HERE.

Ye Knightly Bottom

Ye Fiery Furnace

Unbelievable Revelation!

The sudden major change that was coming over Brat-now-Brassica had not just happened by chance. Nor had it been the situation they had found themselves in that had suddenly made him change from a spoilt little brat to someone with a maturity and wisdom way beyond his eleven or twelve years. Most people learn nothing by experience and if they do, it usually happens too late anyway.

What *had* happened was that when he had been forced to try to free the False Excalibur and the ground had opened up and swallowed him, something incredible had happened.

Others before him who had grasped the fake sword had not met such a generous fate as Brassica. The Spirits of the Kingdom, who were the guardians of the true sword, usually converted the fake sword graspers into little bits of burnt charcoal that were ground up and added to the boiling lava at the centre of the world. This should have been Brassica's fate, but as the spirits began to toast him,[63]

---

[63] *Not in a good 'for he's a jolly good fellow' way, but in an 'anyone fancy a toasted snack?' sort of way.*

223

they realised he was no ordinary person.

There was royal blood in his veins![64]

As soon as they realised this, the Spirits of the Kingdom turned off the gas and spat Brassica out as quickly as they could. They felt rather bad at having nearly toasted the child so to make up for it, they put a lot more extremely clever brain cells inside his head, and that is how he suddenly became much more grown-up and noble.

No, there had not been a terrible miscarriage of justice. Brassica was not the true King Arthur, but he did share his blood.

Brassica who had been Brat who had been the Pretend King Arthur was actually the real King Arthur's half brother.

They were both the sons of Uther Pendragon, but Brassica had a different mother. Arthur's father had not been unfaithful to his wife. He had just mistaken her for her identical twin sister – Bladwyn the Lady of the Leek – who had been so ashamed that she had cast her newborn baby adrift in a wicker basket where he

---

[64] *Yeah! How about that! Bet you never saw that coming!*

had been found by the peasants who had raised him as their own except they hadn't because the second Bladwyn had turned her back, a mysterious unknown secret person had swapped her baby with King Arthur, thus causing this incredibly complicated paragraph that you have just read.[65]

The biggest question, the answer of which could rewrite history or at least give it an upset stomach, was – who was the oldest, King Arthur or Brassica. For surely, being the son of the same King, then the true King of Avalon would be the eldest child. No one knew the answer to this question.[66]

Of course, Brassica had not got the slightest inkling of any of this. No one, apart from the Spirits of the Kingdom, who never spoke to anyone, knew about this. Of course, Bladwyn the Lady of the Leek knew King Arthur had a half brother or sister – she

---

[65] *I realise this should probably be in a footnote, but it is* **MUCH TOO IMPORTANT** *for that. And I'm writing this book, so I can make up the rules.*

[66] *Someone somewhere does know, but whether we will ever find out will remain a mystery until it might be really good in a future book. Or not.*

had been too shy to look before she had wrapped him up and set him adrift – but she was far too ashamed to say anything and not only that, she had become one of those nuns in a monastery where no one is allowed to speak. She never allowed herself to think about her lost child, but if she had, she would probably have assumed he had not survived to adulthood having been eaten either by some river creature or by the peasants who might have pulled his wicker basket from the water. Now and then she had a daydream that her baby had been rescued by a noble lady who had brought it up as her own in the lap of luxury, but she knew that sort of thing only happened in stories. Being a nun in a very, very remote monastery she hadn't heard about one half-brother replacing the other, otherwise she would have known exactly what had happened to her long lost baby and that her child actually had been a boy.

And of course, whoever it was who had swapped the two babies over also knew who Brassica was.

Brassica himself did not have a clue.

They drifted slowly down the lake towards the River Stycks that would carry them away to freedom. Clouds that had offered complete darkness also drifted

away and the lake was bathed in cool blue moonlight. Overhead, Camelot's vampires flew backwards and forwards over the islands searching for the escapees. It was assumed they had taken refuge on land.

'They wouldn't be so stupid as to try and escape by boat while we are out searching for them,' said Merlin. 'They will find an island with shelter and lie low for a few days until we call off the search.'

'Unless they have already reached the far side of the lake and escaped into the forest,' said Sir Lancelot.

'That's true,' said Merlin. 'We will send soldiers and bloodhounds to search the shore.'

Four boatloads were sent each with thirty soldiers and three rabid bloodhounds who hadn't caught a convict for months and were drooling for a snack. One boat sailed within five metres of Brassica and Princess Floridian as they lay stock still beneath their disguise of broken branches.

'What's that?' said a voice on the soldier's boat.

'Just some old branches,' said another.

'Shall I fire a burning arrow into it, just in case?' said a third voice.

'I wouldn't have thought it would burn.'

'It's worth a go.'

A flaming arrow flew across the water. It missed the escapees' boat by a few inches before crash-landing on a small island and setting the whole thing on fire.

'Oops.'

A figure came flying out of the flames and threw itself into the water in a cloud of burning leaves and smoke with a side order of screams.

'I surrender,' the figure cried.

'Bullseye!' cried the first soldier. 'We are in for a big reward.'

'Or not,' whispered Princess Floridian as they drifted further away into the shadows.

The burning man was a runaway who had fled to the island five years earlier before he could be arrested for creeping into farmers' fields at night and carving their vegetables into silly shapes. The trouble was, the things he carved were so horrible that no one wanted to eat the carrots afterwards, so they were all wasted.[67] Then he had moved to turnips, but when he had started working with marrows, the people had got angry and set a trap

---

[67] *The things he carved were probably quite rude, but because this is a children's book, I'm not allowed to say that.*

for him. Apart from depriving them of valuable food, some of the carvings gave people very rude nightmares. Eventually the villagers set a trap to catch him. One night the smallest man in the village hid inside a hollowed-out marrow and waited. When he was found the next morning his eyes were bulging out of their sockets and he was gibbering and a giant rabbit had been painted on his naked body with blue paint. The Vegetable Interferer had struck, but the experience had scared him away and he was never seen again. Until now, when he was hauled out of the lake by the soldiers.[68]

All the confusion with the burning island and the Vegetable Interferer allowed Brassica and his accomplices to slip away behind another island and hide there out of sight until the sailors had reached the other side of the lake.

As dawn rose the next morning Brassica could see a gap in the trees around the lake that showed them the entrance to the river.

---

[68] *The man who had hidden inside the marrow gradually recovered, though whenever he went near onions his eyes would water uncontrollably, a curse that his descendants still endure to this very day.*

229

Three Villains

'They have given us the slip, my lord,' said the captain of the guard when the soldiers arrived back at Camelot after a night's fruitless searching.

'You found no clues as to their whereabouts at all?' said Sir Lancelot.

'Nothing, sire.'

'Methinks your searching was less than thorough,' said Morgan le Fey.

'No, my lady, we searched high and low,' said the captain. 'We looked behind every rock and under every bush. We even apprehended three other criminals.'

'Bring them forth,' said Merlin. 'Perhaps they saw something.'

The three villains were brought in. First there was the Vegetable Interferer dressed in a potato sack and shackled to him was the second criminal, the notorious Road Thief. The Road Thief had topped the charts as Avalon's Most Wanted for as long as anyone could remember and his capture took the immediate pressure off the captain for his failure to find Brassica and Princess Floridian.

The Road Thief was exactly what his name

suggested. He stole roads. People would set off in the early morning for a distant town, riding along in their horse and carriage down a busy road when suddenly, they would turn a corner and the road had vanished. Where there had been well-worn wheel tracks, nice potholes full of rain and cast-off rubbish such as broken pig's bladders[69] and copies of last week's *Ye Avalon Morning Herald* along the roadside, there would be a wide expanse of soft green grass and a few grazing sheep. The road that had been there the night before had simply vanished. Naturally, this was put down to Ancient Magic, but in fact it was the work of one man with a big shovel – The Road Thief. In the middle of the new field there would always be a small sign bearing the words:

Turning Back Man's Destructive Progress

Another Elysian Fields Project

From the Road Thief

---

[69] *The medieval equivalent of a thermos flask.*

The third villain was the blacksmith who was wanted for selling fake steel underpants that were made out of painted canvas and were far more comfortable than the buyers had wanted. There was also the matter of the international turnip smuggling.

'Whilst we are delighted to have apprehended you three,' Merlin said, 'none of you are the reason our soldiers were scouring the lake.'

He went on to explain who they had been looking for and added, 'So if any of you three know something that might help us find our runaways, it would be very good news for you. Were it to lead to their re-capture, it would not only wipe out your crimes completely, but even set you up for life with a weekly potato allowance, a small cottage and a bonus cuddly puppy.'

'I can help you,' said the blacksmith, 'though in doing so I must admit that I have been a stupid fool who was completely taken in.'

He told them how he had freed Brassica and the Princess from their shackles, and even given them weapons before sending them off with his only son.

'Whom I now fear they may have murdered,' he said.

233

'So you have heard nothing since they left?'

'Not a word, nor has my trained hawk been able to find a trace of them,' said the blacksmith.

'Can I assume,' said the Road Thief with a tinge of sadness in his voice, 'that I am no longer Avalon's Most Wanted?'

'You can indeed,' said Merlin. 'Which of course means your punishment will be far less extreme. You will spend five years building new roads, but now you will be allowed to use a shovel.'

Then everyone put their heads together to work out where the runaways might have run away to. This is what they came up with:

- They could be hiding on one of the more than three hundred islands waiting for things to die down.
- They could be hiding on several of the more than three hundred islands waiting for things to die down.
- They could have landed on the far side of the lake and headed for the hills.
- They could have landed on the near side of the lake and headed for the valleys.

- They could have even come back to Camelot and be hiding right under everyone's noses.
- They could have flown off to distant lands on a dragon.
- They could have turned themselves into fishes and be hiding at the bottom of the lake.
- They could have turned themselves into ants that could swim really, really well and be hiding inside a water lily flower.

The final list had eighty-seven possibilities, but, unlike the ones above, most of them were very silly.

'And of course, you have missed out what I think most likely,' said the blacksmith, 'and that is they have sailed away down the river.'

'There's a river?' said several people.

'Is is not guarded by River Sprites?' said Morgan le Fey.

'It is,' said the blacksmith, 'but supposing they did not kill my beloved Rampart? Supposing they forced him to guide them to freedom?'

'So?'

'I do not wish to say more,' said the blacksmith,

235

'for fear of incriminating myself.'

'Fear not, my good fellow,' said Merlin. 'Your help has already earned you the potato allowance and the small cottage. You only have the cuddly puppy to go.'

'Well, as you have suggested, though, of course, I am totally denying it, I might have been ferrying turnips down the river as a favour for a complete stranger I met in an alehouse,' said the blacksmith. 'Well, if I had done that, I would probably have taken my beloved son with me and we would probably have bribed the River Sprites and befriended them. So if that was the case, which of course it isn't, then they would have no problem entering the river.'

'There is also the possibility,' said Morgan le Fey, 'of your son not so much being dead or forced at knifepoint as being a willing member of their gang.'

'What!' cried the blacksmith. 'My beloved Rampart an evil crinimul? He would never leave me. I have given him everything.'

When he was asked to define everything, running away seemed like a better option.

'Very well, let us assume they plan to flee

downriver,' said Merlin. 'I will take preventative measures.'

He took his most powerful wand, the one he only used when things needed enormous magic, and climbed to the top of his Special Spells Tower. Turning towards the window that faced the direction where the river lay, he began to chant.

Sail Away

As the boat drifted towards the river's entrance, Rampart threw the branches that had been hiding them overboard. The water began to move faster now as it was channelled into the narrow opening. The boat picked up speed then stopped dead. The water frothed and raced past them, but they stayed still as if stuck fast to something.

'What's happening?' said Princess Floridian.

'Don't worry, it's the River Sprites,' said Rampart.

'River Sprites?' said Brassica. 'Will they harm us?'

'No, they are my friends. I have been this way with my father many times before,' said Rampart.

The water round the boat fell as flat as glass while a few metres away it still raced like a mad water-dragon. Three pale figures rose from the clear water, one in front of the boat and one at each side.

'Who wishes to pass?' said the first sprite.

'It's me, Rampart.'

'Oh, our young turnip friend,' said the sprite. 'And who are your companions?'

'Just two of my good friends,' said Rampart. 'You wouldn't know them.'

239

The largest of the three River Sprites drifted closer and peered at them.

'The girl we do not know,' said the creature and, looking at Brassica, added, 'but your majesty, though we have never met, it is an honour to let you pass.'

The three ghostly figures slipped back beneath the water and the boat drifted into the river.

'What did he mean by "your majesty"?' said Rampart.

Brassica was about to say that he reckoned they still thought he was the King and hadn't heard about him being deposed, but the air, which had been calm and quiet, was suddenly filled with a deafening roar.

'What on earth is that?' said Princess Floridian.

'I haven't the faintest idea,' said Rampart. 'I have been this way many times, but I have never heard it before.'

Far back across the lake in his tall tower, Merlin put his powerful wand back in its lead-lined cupboard and went back downstairs for a cup of tea and a turnip biscuit.

'If I didn't know better,' Rampart continued as their boat rapidly began to pick up speed, 'I would say

240

it was the sound of the greatest waterfall the world has ever seen, 'cept there aren't any waterfalls anywhere on this river.'

They rounded the bend and raced into a cloud of ferocious, wild, angry, savage, merciless water and there, a hundred metres ahead of them, was the greatest waterfall the world had ever seen.

'That wasn't there last time I came down here,' Rampart said.

'Oh my @@#*** !!!ing ##**,' screamed Brassica, but no one could hear him, which was probably good considering how rude it was.

'HEEEEELLLPPPPPPP . . .' screamed Princess Floridian.

The boat began racing very, very fast.

And then, as suddenly as the racing had begun, it stopped and they were floating in a soft white cloud.

'Thank goodness,' said Rampart.

True, they had stopped being thrown around by the angry water.

True, they were now floating in a soft white cloud.

But it was also true that the floating was more of a falling downwards very, very quickly . . .[70]

---

[70] *I only hope I can write* The Dragons 3 *quickly enough to save them.*

Postscript

'So did you get one?' said Sir Lancelot.

'Get one what?' said his squire Grimethorpe.

'A Troth,' said the knight. 'I would fain pledge one to my beloved Morgan le Fey ere this night is out.'

'I thought I explained about all that, my lord.'

'Oh yes, so you did.'

'I did get flowers and choccies, though, my lord,' said Grimethorpe. 'And if I am not mistaken, my lady waits without.'

'Without? Without what?' said Sir Lancelot.

'Without flowers and choccies.'

'Ah, right, excellent. Hand them over and I shall go without this instant and get plighting.'

Which roughly translated means that just after the three runaways fell over the waterfall, Sir Lancelot and Morgan le Fey got engaged to be married.

Post Postscript

Good result all round, really.

Post-Post-Postscript

Yes, I know we were all expecting Fremsley the Royal Whippet to star in this book. I certainly was. BUT the thing is, whippets are notoriously lazy and by the time Fremsley had got out of bed I had finished writing the whole thing. I would like to be able to tell you that he will appear in *The Dragons 3*, but I can't guarantee it.

FIVE LOVELY, EXCITING, RUDE AND DANGEROUS FATES WORSE THAN DEATH.

① Diving **TOO RUDE!** y naked.

② Kissing **TOO SLIMY!** ellyfish.

③ Putt **TOO GROSS!** th ears.

④ Takin **JUST TOO MUCH FUN!** h hands and s it's wet.

⑤ **ACTUALLY ILLEGAL**

AMAZING COMPETITION!

Become **INCREDIBLY FAMOUS!**
You could even win the Nobel Prize for Thinking.

In *The Floods 10*, Maldegard Ankle-Flood and Edna Hulbert are making the first ever map of Transylvania Waters – and because most of the places are mostly called Here or Over There, they had to come up with names for not just the towns and villages, but the rivers and mountains and tall bits and streets.

All you have to do is think of a name for the capital city of Transylvania Waters.

If you win, you will get a complete signed set of The Floods books and your name will be published in *The Floods 10*. There will also be five runners-up, who will each get a signed copy of *The Floods 10* and their names in the book too.

AND there is a FREE gift for everyone who enters . . .
all the air you can breathe for the Rest Of Your Life!

REMEMBER: Floodstown and Nerlinville are obvious and obvious is **BORING** and will **NOT** win anything except perpetual scorn – though of course if you are reading The Floods books, then you are already quite not boring. **GROSS IS GOOD.** The Judge's – oh what a surprise, that's me – decision will be final and may well be extremely unfair.

Visit **WWW.THEFLOODS.COM.AU** to enter!
Entries close 31 October 2010. Terms and conditions available online.

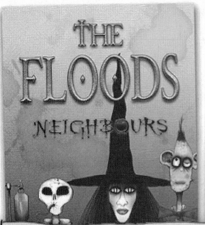

THE FLOODS
NEIGHBOURS

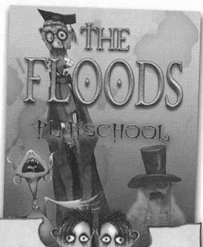

THE FLOODS
PLAYSCHOOL

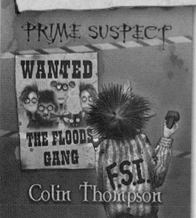

PRIME SUSPECT

WANTED
THE FLOODS GANG
F.S.I.

Colin Thompson

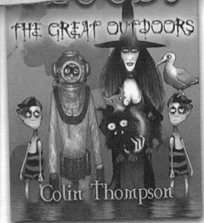

THE GREAT OUTDOORS

Colin Thompson

THE
FLOODS
HOME & AWAY

THE
FLOODS
SURVIVOR

THE
FLOODS
WHO WANTS TO BE
A BILLIONAIRE?

Colin Thompson

$Colin Thompson$

THE
FLOODS
TOP GEAR

Colin Thompson

THE
FLOODS
BETTER HOMES
& GARDENS

Turn to the next page to find out
how you can keep helping . . .